The Love of Julia

Sarah Thompson

The Love of Julia

Sarah Thompson

Published in Canada by Engen Books, St. John's, NL.

Library and Archives Canada Cataloguing in Publication

Title: The love of Julia / Sarah Thompson.
Names: Thompson, Sarah, 1982- author.
Description: Series statement: The Northbeach romances ; 2
Identifiers: Canadiana (print) 20210127872 | Canadiana (ebook) 20210127929 |
ISBN 9781774780138
    (softcover) | ISBN 9781774780121 (PDF)
Classification: LCC PS8639.H639 L67 2021 | DDC C813/.6—dc23

This book is a work of fiction. Names, characters, places and incidents are
products of the author's imagination or are used fictitiously. Any resemblance
to actual events or locales or persons living or dead is entirely coincidental.

Distributed by:
Engen Books
www.engenbooks.com
submissions@engenbooks.com

First mass market paperback printing: January 2021

Cover Design: Matthew LeDrew

For Josh and Daniel
who push me to be a better artist.
Our bubble kept me sane.

Also, for Pop.
He would have hated it,
but he would have "watched" every word.

CHAPTER 1

For Steph Underwood, her career was everything and came ahead of almost anything else in her life. She had spent the morning in a huge fight that potentially meant the end of her five-year relationship, but that was secondary. No matter her feelings about it, she had dragged herself into her boss's office 15 minutes early that evening because he wanted to talk.

She had been sitting on the floor, crying and waiting for something to change when her boss texted her to say that they needed to meet. She had almost forgotten that Jamie was going to be announcing his replacement this evening. The entire staff was set to meet at six o'clock to find out who would get to move into the big office and take over the position of editor-in-chief now that Jamie was just a couple of months away from retirement.

Steph felt as though he had been grooming her to take over the position for years, but there were several other senior reporters and editors that were just as qualified, so it wasn't a guarantee. For a minute she was grateful for Nicole choosing to break things off today. At least it provided a good distraction to keep Steph from thinking about work that evening. She could only hope that work would now provide the same distraction from her personal life.

Steph was always very good at compartmentalizing her feelings so all she felt was nervous energy as she pulled into the parking garage at the North Beach Observer. She took the stairs to the office on the fourth floor to burn off some of the intensity of the feeling and almost ran the first two flights. She was slightly out of breath and decided to take it a little slower the rest of the way so no one would be able to tell when she reached the top.

Steph took a minute to adjust her suit jacket before knocking on the door that read editor-in-chief. Her hand had barely landed back at her side when the door swung open and Jamie grinned at her from ear to ear as he gestured for her to come in.

He quickly sat in the guest chair and invited her to move behind the desk. "Get used to looking at people from that side," He chuckled.

Steph raised one eyebrow in confusion. "Ahh....Does that mean what I think it means?"

"If you think it means I'm promoting you as my replacement, then yes. It means exactly what you think it means."

Steph could feel her jaw drop but could only manage to blink at Jamie. Although she had hoped this was why he wanted to meet with her before she started her workday, she had convinced herself that the real reason was so he could let her down gently.

"Are you going to say anything?" Jamie was still grinning at her overwhelmed reaction.

"I don't know what to say. Thank you. Thank you so much for this opportunity. I will work harder than ever to make sure I show you that you made the right choice." Steph made her way around the desk to shake his hand.

"I know you will. Now, we still have a few minutes before this goes public. You should call that girlfriend of yours and tell her the good news." Jamie patted Steph on the back.

The shocked reaction on Steph's face rivaled the one she had a moment before with the news of her promotion. "My...my...um..."

"Steph, really. We have been working together for eight years. Did you think I wouldn't figure it out? I'm an investigative journalist for Christ's sake. Besides, no one your age has a roommate for five years. Short term, sure, but you guys are so obvious."

"Well, I guess it doesn't matter anymore, anyway. She left me this morning."

"I'm sorry. You seemed so happy. She even brought you that lovely meal when you worked late last night. I had no idea you were having trouble."

"You weren't supposed to have any idea we were a thing," Steph sighed. "I didn't know we were having trouble either."

"Maybe you two can work it out? Find a way to get past whatever is it that made her leave?"

"I don't think so. I think she really meant it. It's my own fault. Besides, it might be good for me to be on my own for a while."

"Well, if you need anything, you know where to find me. In the meantime, let's get out there and fill everyone else in on the good news."

Steph adjusted her jacket again and bent to tie her sneaker before following Jamie out of the office and into the conference room across the hall. She tried desperately to contain a grin as she took her usual place at the table and her co-workers filtered into the room.

The level of chatter was increasing as the room started to fill and Jamie quickly excused himself after a quick check of his cell phone, delaying the start of the meeting. One of the newer junior reporters nervously took a seat beside Steph at the table, scribbling notes on a legal pad.

Julia shot quick glances at Steph as they waited and just as Jamie re-entered the room, she willed enough courage to speak, "I love your outfit," she blushed and went back to her notes as the other reporters quieted down around them.

Steph blushed a little as well, wondering why Julia had sounded so nervous to give her a simple compliment. They had worked together on a couple of stories and even went out for drinks a few times after work, but the girl from those moments never sounded nervous. In fact, she seemed to exude nothing but confidence, even overconfidence at times. She was still focused on the redness of Julia's cheeks and her shy smile when applause suddenly filled the room and she heard Jamie calling for her. Steph quickly shook her previous thoughts from her mind and stood to speak to the group of people that she would soon be taking charge of.

"Well, folks, I can't really say that I saw this coming. There are so many talented leaders in this room, and I just think myself grateful to work amongst all of you. I have a five-year plan for the development of this paper, and I look forward to talking with each and every one of you about your goals for the future and your thoughts about the plan." Steph had a five-year plan for every aspect of her life. She unbuttoned her jacket and placed her hand on her hip. "I know there are a number of you who are disappointed that this role has not been offered to you, but I assure you that I will treat you all as my equals as we move forward as a team. Thank you."

Julia quickly averted her eyes and grinned as Steph sat back down beside her at the conference table. Steph's face was flushed from the adrenaline of speaking in front of the group, and still a little red from her interaction with Julia beforehand. She couldn't help but sneak small glances at the girl beside her throughout the rest of the meeting and wonder why she was suddenly so embarrassed to look at her.

The pair remained seated as the rest of the team filtered out of the room a few minutes later, both lost in their own thoughts and continuing to steal small glances at each other. Jamie finished clearing up the papers spread out before him, tapping the stack on the desk and clearing his throat to encourage them back to reality.

Steph stood up quickly, knocked her notes to the floor and scrambled to pick them up before rushing out the door and back to her office. She couldn't shake the feeling that Julia might have been flirting with her and it was throwing her off her game. Any other day she wouldn't have even considered that was what she had intended, but now that she was to become the boss, she was looking at their interactions a little differently. Even if it wasn't just wishful thinking that Julia was interested, Steph knew there couldn't be anything between them. Besides, she wasn't even 12 hours removed from a huge fight with Nicole and she hadn't even really processed what that meant.

Nicole. She had actually packed a bag and walked out the door. She said it was over between them. She said there was nothing Steph could do to make her change her mind. After just a couple of hours at work, Steph wasn't even sure that she wanted Nicole to change her mind anymore. She started to wonder if she had, in some way, been slowly trying to push Nicole away. She was choosing to take extra shifts at work, even when she knew it was Nicole's day off and she ignored Nicole's pleas for them to go out and do more things together. The more she thought about it, the more she realized how little of her time and energy she had been giving Nicole over the last couple of months. It wasn't because she didn't love her, she was sure of that, but Steph hated to argue with anyone about anything, and it seemed like that was all they did anymore.

Steph looked up to find Julia standing in her doorway, practically staring at her as she remained lost in thought. "Something you need?" Steph felt her voice drop to her flirting tone as she spoke although she didn't mean to.

Julia giggled at the intonation in Steph's words. "Not really. Just wondered why you seem so off today. You haven't been yourself since you came in. Also, I wanted to actually say congrats on the promotion. I never did say the words."

"Umm, yeah, thanks." Steph tried to ignore the first part of Julia's comment.

"And about you seeming off?" Julia pried, moving into the office and sitting on the edge of Steph's desk.

"It's nothing," Steph shrugged. She and Julia had been working toward a friendship over the last several months, but she had been pulling away from it lately as Julia was a co-worker and she didn't want to let her in on too much of her personal life.

"C'mon, Steph. You know you can talk to me about whatever it is. I thought we were starting to get close." Julia tapped her pen against Steph's desk. "Like, actual friends, you know? It just feels like you are blocking me out here and something is really bothering you."

"It's really none of your business. Besides, we can't

be friends, not really. Not now that I'm going to be your boss."

"Why not? I don't think there are any rules about it. We were friends before you got the promotion, I don't know what the big deal is." Julia absentmindedly cracked her knuckles as she wondered if she should push harder for an answer. She took a deep breath. "You know, you can tell me it is none of my business until the cows come home, but I can promise you that just makes me more sure there is something big happening with you and that you probably need a friend right now."

Steph felt a wave of embarrassment flood over her. "Maybe I should just say that I'm not ready to talk about it. I don't really mean to shut you out. It just seems like this entire day has been filled with anger and fighting and now...I think I am taking it out on you."

"Who are you fighting with? More and more I realize that as much time as we spend together at the office, I don't know anything about your life. Boyfriend troubles?" Julia raised one eyebrow.

Steph shook her head no and lowered her eyes, staring at her hands, folded in her lap.

"Girlfriend troubles, then?" Julia smiled knowingly.

"Does everybody know?" Steph sighed.

Julia laughed, "I don't think anybody else is on to you, but I don't know what you are so worried about. No one is going to care. It's 2007 and people in this business are pretty liberal these days. Besides, I only know because I tend to recognize my own kind," Julia said with a wink.

"Your own...oh!" Steph blushed again. She hadn't been completely crazy to think Julia might be flirting with her.

"So, are you going to fill me in on your drama or what?"

"There isn't much to tell. My girlfriend of half a decade packed a bag and walked out on me before I left for work today, so there's that."

"You seem pretty calm about it."

"Not much I can do about it. I guess I should have seen it coming, but I really didn't. She says we have the same fight all the time. Maybe it hasn't sunk in yet, but maybe I just don't care that it's over." Steph rubbed the back of her neck beneath her ponytail.

"I'm sure that isn't true. You wouldn't have been together for five years if you didn't care. You just have a lot going on right now." Julia rubbed her hand down Steph's arm. "I just want to say this, not to be corny or anything, but I think you know that I'm here for you if you need someone to talk to or anything."

"I appreciate that, but I'm going to be just fine. Besides, Nicole leaving might have just been anger. I'm not sure that she won't be back. Maybe that's why I'm not upset about it. Or maybe I'm glad and I can't accept that yet."

"It could just be a big fight. Maybe you guys will be able to talk it out once she cools down. Has she ever walked out on you like that before?"

"Early on, once or twice, but I always chased her and got her to sit down and talk about things. She was just so calm about it all. Her words seemed so controlled and calculated. Usually, I have to be the relaxed one that puts things in perspective. Today it was all her." Steph bowed her head starting to realize that Nicole's words were probably practiced. "I think she has been planning this for a while."

"It's possible. Especially if what you are saying is true and she seemed out of character from your other fights."

Julia took her by the hand, giving her an understanding smile. "I meant it when I said I would be here for you."

"I know you did. Enough of me feeling sorry for myself, though. We should get back to work. It's going to be another busy day in the news." Steph pulled her hand away and turned back to her computer.

CHAPTER 2

"Hey you! I'm starting to think you are avoiding me!" Julia ran up to the elevator in the parking garage of the North Beach Observer office and paused behind Steph with a look of pity on her face. She hadn't laid eyes on the new boss since the announcement was made three days ago.

"Oh, hey. No, not avoiding you per se, just avoiding everyone the past few days. It has been a lot of work to get up to speed on taking over for Jamie before he leaves, and it has been weird to be in that big house alone."

Julia placed her hand on Steph's lower back, "Nicole still hasn't come home?"

Steph shivered a little at Julia's touch. She was still getting used to how often Julia found a way to be in physical contact with her when they spoke. She had tried to take notice when Julia interacted with some of the other reporters, and it seemed like this was just something Julia did out of habit, rather than something special, just for her. "Nope. And she won't answer my texts or calls. The only thing I have heard from her since she left is that she will be coming by tonight to pick up some more of her stuff. I did tell her that I'm working the day shift this week, but I don't know if she remembers that, or if she thinks tonight is a good time because I will be working. Maybe I'll just stay late anyway so I don't have to see her."

"Or, maybe she does know that you are on days and she is coming tonight so that you can talk. If I were you, I would make sure that I was there when she came by. If you want any chance of working this out, that is." Julia kept her hand in place to guide Steph onto the elevator.

"Can we just talk about something else? I don't want to start the day worrying about what is going to happen when I get home." Steph said, struggling to keep her attention away from the fact that Julia was still touching her. She didn't generally like it when people were in her personal space, but she was having a 'hands meeting in the popcorn' moment where she didn't want to do anything to make the contact end.

Julia pulled her hand from Steph's back and folded her arms across her chest. "Sure, we can talk about whatever you want. How about that open editor position? Have you decided who you are going to promote to fill your shoes?" The speed of Julia's words increased as she continued. "Keeping in mind that I am not asking because I think I am in the running. The last thing I want to do is become an editor just yet."

Steph couldn't help but chuckle a little. "I haven't made any decisions, and I am fully aware that you aren't interested in the job. I do have a couple of people in mind and one person I never even thought about approached me asking to be considered. It might be a couple of days before I get that all in place and of course, then we are going to have to hire someone from the outside to fill at least one position once everyone else is moved around."

"I didn't realize there would be other movement. Guess this one promotion is going to be a lot more work than I would have considered it to be." Julia scratched her head.

"There might be more movement. Depends on who gets my job, I guess. I'm going to be talking to the candidates today. That's as much as I'm going to tell you about it. Wouldn't want it getting around the office that I'm letting a junior reporter in on some of the top secrets." The elevator door binged as they reached the fourth floor and Steph stepped off, head down. Her thoughts drifted back to Nicole as she made her way to her office at the end of the hall.

Steph jumped and almost slammed the door behind her when she turned to see Jamie sitting in the office waiting for her. "Geez, way to sneak up on a girl." Steph quickly wiped a tear from her cheek.

"She still isn't talking to you, I suppose?" Jamie stood and placed his hand on her shoulder, giving it a little squeeze of fatherly reassurance.

"No, and why is this what everyone wants to talk to me about this morning? I haven't even had coffee yet and two people have been pushing me for information about my personal life!" Steph threw her briefcase to the floor and slammed her hands down on the edge of her desk.

"Woah! I don't know who pissed in your corn flakes this morning, but I thought you were handling this well until now. Is it the extra stress of the interviews today that is getting to you? We could put them off. Give it a few more days before making a decision."

"No. I'm sorry. I shouldn't have gone off on you like that. It's just that Julia..." Steph pursed her lips.

"What about Julia?" Jamie ribbed.

"Not like that. She knows is all and she asked me the same thing on the way up from the garage. I don't know how I feel about it and now I might have to get home on time this evening so that I can deal with Nicole in person." Steph took a deep breath. "I don't want to put off the interviews. Let's just get it out of the way so there is one less thing on my plate, okay?"

"Sure thing." Jamie flashed her a pity smile and she glared back, shaking her head.

The day easily flew by for Steph as the parade of candidates for her old job filtered in and out of her office. She also had a lengthy discussion with Jamie about who they would hire and the plan to replace that position in the office. They decided to promote one of the photojournalists and that they would hire that position externally. At ten to five Steph started to tidy her desk and packed a few things that she wanted to work on at home into her briefcase before clicking off the lights and heading out the door for the night.

Steph wasn't sure if she wanted to run into Nicole when she got home or not, but she knew there were still too many things left unsaid between them not to try. She rushed through the door of the empty house and hurried to change into more comfortable clothes. Nicole had always hated when she was wearing a business suit, so she threw on her favourite sweatshirt and jeans and nervously planted herself on the couch, listening and waiting for the door to open.

Steph heard the unmistakable sound of Nicole's key in the lock, hurriedly turned off the television and stood in the porch, waiting for the door to open. She couldn't help but smile a little when Nicole opened the door, but Nicole looked less than impressed to find her there.

"I thought you would be at work. I'll come back another time." Nicole flipped her keys over her finger into her hand and turned to leave.

"No, no. I thought you knew I would be here. I told you I was moving to the nine to five if I got the promotion and I sent you a message to let you know that I did. I know that you haven't been replying to me, but I hoped you were at least reading my messages."

"Truth?" Nicole pocketed the keys and folded her arms across her chest as Steph nodded. "I blocked your number. I wanted to make sure that I didn't know if you tried to contact me. Congrats on the promotion, by the way. I figured you would get it."

"Thanks. I wasn't so sure, but I'm really looking forward to the challenge. I can't believe you blocked me." Steph added quickly.

"I didn't know how else to make sure that I didn't talk to you. You were such a big part of my life for so long. How was I supposed to figure out how to be without you if you were going to try to talk to me?"

"We should be trying to figure this out together, Nic. Everything has changed now. Everything. Turns out I wasn't exactly keeping the best secret anyway."

"Maybe someone will understand, and you can figure it out with them, but I just can't be anyone's secret anymore. I won't. I'm tired of pretending, tired of playing these games and you can say all you want that everything is different now, but it isn't."

Steph cut her off, "I know it isn't really different yet, but the situation has changed, and it is what we have been waiting for, for so long. It will be so much better from here on."

"For you, and for me but not for us, Steph. We really are done. I'm sorry if I made it seem like the secrets and lies to everyone were the only problem. They may have been the underlying issue that compounded everything but you not being out wasn't the only thing that broke us."

"Enlighten me. Because the way I see it, you told me it was over and that it was all because I didn't want people at work to know about my personal life. You said it was because you couldn't handle being my dirty little secret any longer. So, Nicole, enlighten me. What is the real reason that you are walking away from everything that we shared over the last five years?"

"I'm just not in love with you anymore. It really is that simple. Everything that you have put me through, all the lies. Having to have the same fight over and over again it just stole the love from me. I still do love you in a way, but I'm not in love with you anymore. I don't want you like you want me to. I can't be someone who will make you feel the way that you should. I can't give you the attention and affection that you should get out of a relationship. I've tried, God knows I have, but I can't find it within myself anymore. I'm just making both of us miserable and if you actually take some time to feel this, you will know that I'm telling you the truth. But that is part of it too. I don't think you were ever invested in this relationship. Have you even stopped to care that I told you it was over? Or did you do what you always do, push it to the backburner until it was long enough ago that you don't have to feel it?"

"I don't do that, not when it comes to you!" Steph struggled to get a word in edgewise.

"Whether you realize it or not, you do. You do it with everything. I used to think it was a cool skill, something you picked up for survival after showing up at one too many fires or car accidents. Now I think you had the skill first and it's why you are good at what you do."

"So, you're saying that you even have problems with my coping mechanisms? This is getting ridiculous. What is the real answer here? Is there someone else? It has to be for you to be so disconnected so quickly, it's not like you. You acted the same way when you and I hooked up and you left your ex."

"That's not what this is, Steph. I promise you, there is no one else. I think you have already moved on though. I think you may not have been cheating on me, but your heart walked out that door long before I did. Honestly, I think you need to be with someone that is more like you anyway, just the right amount of sociopathic tendency."

"So now you are saying that you think I'm like a serial killer?"

"Just in the way you refuse to feel empathy for most people, or care when you find out someone is dead. You just take it with a grain of salt and move on. Speaking of moving on, I really do need to pick up some clothes and a few things. I don't have a lot of time and I didn't realize I was going to have to deal with this when I got here."

Steph grabbed her by the shoulders and forced Nicole to look her in the eyes. "No matter what you might think, I have never stopped loving you or wanting you." Steph pulled her in and kissed her hard.

Nicole pushed her back, startled, and focused on the hurt in Steph's eyes. A single tear rolled down her cheek and she quickly wiped it away before pulling Steph in and returning the kiss even more aggressively. Before Steph knew what was happening, Nicole had unzipped her hoodie and was reaching to undo her bra.

Without hesitation Steph pulled Nicole's t-shirt over her head and began unbuttoning her jeans as she guided her toward the couch. Nicole watched Steph's hands as they moved along the warmth of her flesh, refusing to let herself make eye contact. Steph pushed her onto the couch and straddled her, falling into rhythm and allowing her hands to move almost on their own as they found the spots she knew would drive Nicole crazy.

Steph slid off Nicole's lap, hooked her fingers into the belt loops of her jeans and pulled them to her ankles before falling to her knees in front of Nicole and softly pressing her lips to her inner thigh. She could already feel the familiarity of it all, the comfort of being with someone for so long and knowing exactly what to do. Steph felt Nicole's muscles begin to tense as she pressed her lips to the soft fabric of the underwear between her legs, already damp with the anticipation of what was to come next.

Nicole groaned as Steph pushed the fabric out of the way and pressed her tongue roughly inside her. Nicole threaded her hand through Steph's hair, tugging ever so gentle and pushing her face deeper between her legs and forcing Steph's tongue just a little deeper inside her.

Steph felt Nicole's hand start to tremble and her grip release as the muscles of her thighs tensed and her legs spread just a little wider before Nicole released a moan that Steph had heard so many times before. She pulled back a little and gently flicked her tongue over Nicole's most sensitive areas before sliding her weight back along Nicole's legs and grinning up at her as Nicole continued to stare at the ceiling and tremble.

Nicole barely took a moment to catch her breath before pushing Steph backward onto the floor and pulling herself down on top of her. She unbuckled Steph's belt with ease, popped open her button and pulled off her jeans, throwing them over the couch Nicole pressed her hand down into her underwear, moving each finger methodically into place and resting her head on Steph's chest to keep from looking up at her.

Nicole knew exactly what to do to make Steph scream with ecstasy and didn't waste any time getting to the point. Steph focused on Nicole's gentle strokes and her breathing increased almost immediately at the touch. Although she tried to hold onto the moment, to make the feeling last just a little longer, her body had other ideas and she soon felt the warm gush of relief and Nicole's hand slide back up her body.

Nicole pulled her body weight from Steph and sat with her back against the couch, staring off at the photos on the wall, still refusing to look at the woman who had been the love of her life for so long.

"This is the wrong time, but I don't know why you would want to walk away from this. We are so good together."

"This was never our problem, Steph." Nicole stood from the floor and searched the room for her clothing. "This, this is the one thing that was always good. The only problem is that sex was almost always the result of a fight. You only show passion with me when you are angry."

"That's so not true!" Steph pulled her shirt back over her head. "It was never about anger! Not even this time. I just wanted to remind you how good we can be together."

"It still isn't going to change my mind. We just don't work overall and we both need to accept that and move on. We both need to find someone to be with that we don't constantly fight with. Someone that we have more in common with than the last five years that we spent together."

"We have more in common than our past, Nic. You

know that as well as I do." Steph stood in her underwear and t-shirt, ready to start another round of pleading.

"Maybe so, but I have changed so much and so have you. We aren't good for each other." Nicole buttoned her jeans and sat on the couch.

"I'm still the same person I always was, and nothing has changed the way I feel about you."

Nicole sighed. "I hate you for the way you make me feel. Like I'm the only person in the world one minute and like I'm invisible and mean nothing to you the next."

"So, what was all this? One more for the road?" Although she hadn't been before, Steph could now feel the anger bubbling up inside her, a feeling like she had just been used.

"I need you to understand that we are really over. I never should have let this happen. I have to get my stuff together and go. I'm going to be moving the rest of my things on the weekend and I would really appreciate it if you would plan to be somewhere else while I do."

"Fine. Get what you need. I'll make sure I'm out of the house all day Saturday, don't worry. I wouldn't want to watch as you destroyed our life together anyway."

CHAPTER 3

On Jamie's last day at the Observer, they had a small party in the conference room where Steph was planning to announce who would be taking over her previous role. She had been stuck between two of her top choices and really didn't want to have the staff think there was any favouritism, so she let Jamie make the final decision.

It had come down to one of their top photojournalists, Matthew Davis, and senior reporter Frank Barnett who had more years on the job but was a more complicated move as they would have to promote internally into the reporter position and then hire a junior from outside. Steph had a closer relationship with Matthew and was afraid it would be perceived as being about their friendship if she was the only one making the decision. In truth, he was just a better editor but with this being the first time she had to make this kind of choice, she was glad that she had Jamie to lean on.

Steph clinked her glass and cleared her throat to get the attention of the room. "Well, I suppose aside from the free food and the chance to have a drink in the workplace, there might be one other reason that you all showed up here this evening." People began to take seats around the conference table as quietly as they could to hear what

Steph had to say. She waited for the movement to cease and looked around at the impatient faces of the four who had applied for her job.

"Okay, don't keep them in suspense any longer Editor-in-Chief. I think they have waited long enough for you to make this decision." Jamie patted her on the shoulder and leaned against the desk beside her.

"Yes, boss. Without further ado, the new senior staff editor will be Matthew Davis. I want to thank the others that applied for the job and I want you to know that this was a very difficult choice. I also want to thank Jamie in helping me to reason through the process. I know that Matthew will do a wonderful job in his new position. I also want to let you know that you are all welcome to apply for Matthew's job in the photo department, but I will also be advertising it externally." Steph watched as some of the junior level reporters shot glances at each other about the news. "Okay, time to get back to celebrating!"

"Speaking of celebrations, how about we have a little one of our own later this evening?" Julia half whispered to Steph across the table. "I heard Nicole picked up the last of her stuff and I figure it would be better to celebrate your newfound singledom rather than let you mope around about it any longer."

"I haven't been moping! Besides, I'm suddenly in my mid-30s and alone, how am I supposed to be acting and feeling?"

"It's been almost a month since she first walked out. She has been slowly collecting her things since that day and she just gave you back the key last night. You are allowed to still be a little upset, but it is time to at least try to go out and have fun. Maybe hook up with someone, maybe don't. Maybe just get out of your head for a night."

"Fine. What did you have in mind?"

"How about a couple of drinks at Leroy's?"

"I don't think so. Thanks for the offer." Steph stood from the table and left the conference room to putter over story ideas in her office.

***

By the end of the week, only one resume was handed in from a current employee and Steph made the decision to send out the open call for applications early the next week. Monday was fairly hectic at the Observer, so it was first thing Tuesday morning before she posted the open call. It was just over an hour later when she received a resume from Kerri Walters at the Jenkinsville Gazette. Steph chuckled to herself when it arrived in her inbox. She had been following Kerri's career since she won a couple of awards the previous year and had been kind of hoping, in the back of her mind, that Kerri would apply.

Steph picked up the phone and called Jamie immediately. "So, you know how I joked that I really wanted to poach that young photographer out in Jenkinsville? Well, you are never going to believe who was the first person to respond to the job posting."

"I might not believe it, but I don't have to guess who you are talking about. Are you going to bother to wait for more applications? You know she is the one you are going to hire," Jamie offered in a fatherly tone.

"I'm probably going to just offer her the job. I want to meet with her first and make sure she is a good fit personality wise, but that is really just a formality. Thoughts?"

"Steph, you know I can't tell you what to do anymore. You have to make this decision for yourself. If you think she is the best applicant you are going to get, make sure she doesn't take a job somewhere else." Jamie sighed.

"Also, it's your paper to run. I didn't give you this job lightly. You don't need my help with this, I swear."

"I know. I just like you to confirm what I already know. I'm going to call her right now. Thanks, Jamie. You're the best."

Steph hung up the phone and opened the resume file to find a number for Kerri. The phone rang twice on Steph's end and she took a deep breath, crafting what she wanted to say in the conversation. She froze for a second when Kerri answered. "Hi Kerri, Steph Underwood. How are you?"

There was a rustling, like brushing of fabric against the receiver before Kerri responded. "I'm doing well, how are you?"

Steph took a deep breath and tried not to express the excitement in her voice, "I just received your resume," she choked, "I was hoping you would be interested in coming into the office for an interview tomorrow?" Steph's mind raced; she didn't mean to call it an interview. It was more of a meet and greet that she had planned.

"An interview? Tomorrow? Sure, yeah. I can be there."

"Excellent. We will see you then." Steph decided she would explain more of the specifics when Kerri arrived and hung up the phone before Kerri had a chance to ask any further questions.

Steph printed Kerri's resume and did a little research to make sure she knew all about the awards she had won most recently. She had wondered on a number of occasions why someone with as much talent as Kerri would be wasting her time working for a small-town gazette and was excited to give her a chance to cut her teeth in a big city.

Steph stacked the papers neatly on her desk and grabbed her sport jacket from the rack in the corner of her office before checking the laces on her sneakers and heading out of the office and down the street to La Bistro.

She sat down at a table near the back and focused her eyes through the darkness on the menu in front of her. She knew what she was going to order, of course. She always ordered the same thing, but she liked to convince herself to read the menu and maybe this time she would have something different.

She smiled up at the waitress as she approached dropping the menu on the table in front of her. "I'm trying not to order the usual." Steph laughed. "What do you think the chances are that I will actually do something different?"

The waitress smiled back and pulled her pad of paper from the apron around her waist. She had served Steph and Nicole a couple of times a few months back, but this was the first time Steph had managed to walk through the doors of La Bistro since they broke up. The waitress tapped her pen on the pad and flipped her hair over her shoulder to reveal her name tag that read Sylvia.

"Well, if you aren't going to go with your usual order, can I at least get you a drink while you ponder the other options?"

"I'll have a beer, I guess. Whatever you have on tap is just fine." Steph picked the menu up from the table as Sylvia nodded and headed back toward the bar.

Julia pushed hurriedly through the door of the restaurant and planted herself on a stool at the bar to await her take out order. Since moving into the apartment above the restaurant she had made it her goal to try everything on the menu at least once. She fiddled with a stack of coasters in front of her and watched the waitress pour a beer from the taps.

"I'll be right with you, hon. I think your order is going to be a couple of minutes."

Julia nodded, "Sure thing. I'm not in a hurry anyway." She watched as the waitress brought the drink to a table in the back and smiled when she recognized the woman, sitting alone in the corner of the restaurant.

Steph took a large swig of the beer and wiped her mouth with the back of her hand. "You know, after all of that, I'm still going to order my usual. But, just to mix it up a little, I'll have the steamed mussels to start." She handed the menu back to Sylvia as she finished jotting down the order and picked up her head to notice Julia waving from the bar.

Steph reluctantly waved back, unsure if she wanted Julia to remain at the bar or offer to join her. She smiled shyly and quickly reached into her briefcase to take another look at Kerri's resume. By the time she located the papers, Julia was standing over her table.

"Fancy meeting you here. I don't think I have seen you eat here before. Do you come here often?" Julia chuckled, "And that sounded like an embarrassingly cheesy pick-up line. Wow. Let me try that again. I moved into the apartment upstairs a couple of months ago and come here almost every night. I didn't realize you liked this place."

Steph could feel her face flush and hoped Julia could not tell how much she was blushing. "I haven't been in a while. I used to bring Nicole here every week. I haven't been back since, you know."

"Well, I was going to take my order to go, but if you would rather not eat alone, I wouldn't mind joining you?"

"I — I guess that would be okay. I suppose there is nothing wrong with sharing a table with a co-worker," Steph stammered.

Julia motioned for the waitress and sat across from Steph at the table. "I guess my order will be for here after all. Might as well order a beer too, I can't have you drinking alone." Julia's dimples popped from her cheeks as she gave Steph a sly smile.

Steph nervously downed her beer, "You better make that two." She shook the empty glass, "I guess I was thirsty."

They sat in silence until Sylvia returned with their beers and the appetizer Steph ordered, barely even making eye contact as they waited. Steph flipped through Kerri's resume and stole glances at Julia as she wiped the condensation from her beer glass and played with the extra coaster on the table. When the main course arrived, Julia finally built up the nerve to speak.

"Thanks for letting me join. I know you said that it could be weird for us to hang out outside of work now that you are the big boss." Julia dipped her chin to her chest and glanced up for Steph's reaction.

Steph sat, her jaw dropped, searching for any words to make the situation less awkward. "Well, I just, I mean, I'm just thinking about how other people might perceive us spending time together. I wouldn't want anyone to think that I was picking favourites or anything."

"C'mon Steph, you know people wouldn't think that. They all know you too well for that to be the case. I think you are just afraid they might think there is something more between us." Julia's expression changed from annoyance to shock, "I didn't mean to say that!" She managed to choke out.

"Yes, you did. But that isn't true. There isn't anything more between us than co-workers and, on some level, maybe friends. Besides, I have done everything I can to keep my personal life to myself, so there is no reason that anyone would think there was something more to my spending time with another woman."

Julia grasped on to the bravery that had made her speak up, "Well, maybe it is just wishful thinking on my part, but I got the impression that you like me."

"Well, you should get a different impression. I don't think of you like that. Besides, even if I did, I'm in no way ready to think about anyone in a romantic kind of way." Steph played with the food on her plate, staring intently at it in the fear Julia would see something else in the way she was acting.

"I know that. It's way too soon for you to be interested in anything serious. I wasn't suggesting this was a date or anything. I was just saying that when you are ready, if the timing is right, maybe you would be interested in giving me a chance?" Julia blurted out the words without thinking.

"We talked about this, didn't we? It would be inappropriate for us to see each other socially. Even this, tonight, is a little inappropriate, don't you think?"

"No, I don't think. There is no rule about office romance, if there was, no one we work with would ever get a date. You know what it is like to be a journalist. Crazy hours, long days, skipping meals, chasing accidents. The only people that really understand it are other people that live the life."

"It's fine when you are all on the same level, it's different for me." Steph sighed.

"I disagree, but whatever. You can isolate yourself all

you want, that is your prerogative. Tell me that you really mean it when you say there is nothing between us and I will move on." A lump formed in Julia's throat as she spoke. The tension between them had been building for almost a year around the office, but she never said anything because Steph was so secretive about her life and she was feeling like she had missed her window.

Steph took a moment to compose herself before responding. "There can't be anything between us. There is nothing between us. I enjoy your company, we were starting to build a friendship, but that is all it was. All it can be. You should move on." She could hear a shake of uncertainty in her voice as she spoke.

"Okay. If that's what you want, that is what I will do. But please, don't close off to me altogether. You need a friend right now, and so do I."

"Fine. I can promise you that I won't shut you out." Steph finished her beer and motioned for the waitress to bring the cheque.

CHAPTER 4

Steph arrived at the office an hour early the next morning to prepare the details of the contract she was about to offer Kerri Walters for the photojournalist position. This was the first time she had held an interview on her own and she could feel the beads of sweat forming on the palms of her hands and across her forehead.

Steph could hear shuffling in the office and slid from behind her desk to investigate. "You're here awful early. Something I should know?"

"No. I just wanted to talk to you before the rest of the world arrived. I just wanted to say...about last night..." Julia forced herself to maintain eye contact.

"There is nothing to say. I told you, there is never going to be anything between us. You should cut your losses and move on." Steph wiped her face in her sleeve. "Now, please, can we just pretend none of this ever happened? I have a lot to do today."

Julia nodded. "Sure thing, boss. Just remember that whatever happens next, I'm not going to stop being your friend and it would be great if I could still talk to you like we used to."

Steph's voice softened, "Of course we can. My door is always open for you if you need to talk, especially about work."

"Okay then." Julia turned to walk back to her own office, "I suppose I will see you around."

Steph checked her collar and nervously fixed her hair, constantly looking between the watch on her wrist and the clock on her computer as she awaited Kerri's arrival. She was sure she had paced a hole in the carpet of her office floor over the last hour while she checked and rechecked her plan of what she was going to say.

With just ten minutes until Kerri was to arrive her office phone rang and after looking at the number on the display, she was forced to pick up. Steph clicked record on her computer and put on her best reporter voice as she answered. "Mr. Mayor! I have been trying to get you on the phone for a week. I heard a rumour that you are diverting some additional funds to the creation of a water park in the playground on the west side of town. Just wanted you to comment on whether you think residents will think this a waste of money when half of the city is built on a beach?"

Steph listened intently for a minute or two, trying to find a place to interject in the conversation to ask additional questions. She could see through the window that Kerri had arrived and was now speaking to Julia at the front desk of the Observer. Watching their interaction was distracting her from the interview that had now gone on much longer than she anticipated.

"Well, I guess we will find out at the next council meeting what the people really think of this allocation of funds when they have been screaming for additional road work for the last two years." The comment came off as snarky, even though she didn't mean it to. "Thank you, Mr. Mayor. I appreciate you taking the time to comment on this for me."

Steph hung up the phone and opened the door to her office. She immediately noticed Kerri focusing on her footwear. "It's a fast-paced business. No matter how nice you want to look, you have to be ready to run." She extended her hand and Kerri shook it. "Sorry to keep you waiting. I didn't know the mayor would be so long winded, but you know how it is when you are trying to get the scoop. Nice to finally meet you, Kerri. Why don't you come in?"

Kerri took a seat in the office and fussed with her briefcase, pulling out both the physical portfolio and the CD-ROM and laying it on the desk. "I brought a number of different samples of my work." She reached into her briefcase again. "And here is a hard copy of my CV. I know it isn't much to look at, being that I have had the same job since I graduated, but that is exactly why I would be perfect for this job."

Steph laughed nervously. "I should have been clearer on the phone. The interview is just a formality. I am familiar with your work. Three award nominations in five years on the job will get you quite a bit of attention. I was very surprised when you applied for our opening as you were doing so well in Jenkinsville, but I am excited to have you join the team."

Kerri just stared back at Steph. "You mean, you're offering me the job?"

Steph nervously started running through the list of points she had compiled to talk to Kerri about. "That's right. I wanted you to come in to talk about what your responsibilities would be and when you are able to start. We have company apartments that you can move into as early as next week until you find a place of your own."

Steph smiled as she watched Kerri's foot nervously tap

against the floor while she pressed her palms on her knees to try to stop the shaking. Then Kerri scratched her head, "Well, I would have to give a week of notice, at least. So, I could start a week from Monday?"

Steph made a couple of adjustments to the information she had put together for the contract that morning. "That will work just fine. I will have someone in legal draw up the contract and we will fax it out to you in a couple of days. I'll also send you all the details about the apartment, including your rental rate and we will see you in just over a week." Steph smiled.

Kerri stood and reached to shake her hand once again. "Thank you. This is such an amazing opportunity, and I can't wait to get started." She quickly packed her things back into her briefcase and headed to the door. "Thank you again."

Steph sighed with relief as Kerri closed the door behind her. The interview didn't go as poorly as she had anticipated and there was little to debate in the contract as Kerri had seemed extremely eager to move to the city. Steph started to pace around the office again before heading out into the break room to attempt to burn off some of the nervous energy she was feeling.

Steph walked with her head down, trying to keep people from seeing the stupid grin she was sporting and ran directly into Julia, also grinning to herself and walking with her face buried in her Blackberry.

"Oh god, I'm so sorry. I should have been watching where I was going," Steph apologized without even knowing who she had banged into.

"It's my fault, really. I should have been paying less attention to my phone and more to where I was going. I was just getting excited because it looks like I have a date tonight!"

"That was fast," Steph sneered. Sure, she had told Julia to move on, but she hadn't really expected it to be this fast. "Didn't waste any time on that one. It's not the new girl that I was interviewing this morning, is it?"

Julia chuckled. "No, I don't work that fast. I mean, she was really cute and all, but I barely said ten words to the girl. This is just someone I met online."

"You're dating on the internet? Don't you worry that you'll wind up meeting psychos? I don't think I would be able to meet up with randoms like that."

"It's not as bad as it seems, and you get to know a little bit about the person before you meet. I find it kinda cool that I already know if we have anything in common before we ever have to interact. It makes the small talk a little easier at the very least." Julia looked up at the clock on the breakroom wall. "I suppose I should get back to work. The police are going to give a statement about the murder later today," Julia had been working the Closet murder case all week. So far, police had found the bodies of two women in their apartments after they had spent the evening at the local gay bar, The Closet. The first one was just over a year ago but this one was so similar that Julia was sure they were connected and that it was a much bigger story than police were currently saying. "So, I should catch up on some other things to clear my schedule for that. Besides, I don't think you want to know about the people I'm dating," Julia added.

"Yeah, okay. You go ahead and do that. And, no, I probably don't want to hear about whomever you are going out with tonight." Steph turned her back and muttered under her breath, "Or any night for that matter." She composed herself and turned back to Julia, "But I suppose I will have to if we are going to make this friends thing work. I really do want to try to be friends, as long as it doesn't impact our work relationship. I was thinking about it, and you're right. No one is going to think there is any favouritism from my end if we are friends. I'm just so paranoid about being the boss for the first time. I want everything to be perfect."

"You haven't been acting like much of a friend. Even just now, you are acting like you are mad at me." Julia shook her head.

"I'm not very good at making and keeping friends. But you were right when you said I really need one right now. It would seem Nicole got all of our friends in the breakup. It's been a little lonely, I have to admit. And this is also the first time in eight years that I have been single."

"One of those serial monogamists, are you?"

"I didn't intend to be, it just sort of worked out that way. I was with someone for a few years and that relationship kind of overlapped with Nicole. So, I find myself almost a decade later wondering if I even know how to go on a date, or flirt or anything," Steph stuttered.

"Oh, you know exactly how to flirt. In fact, I think you flirt with everyone, whether you are intending to or not." Julia laughed.

"Really? I mean, people have called me a big flirt in the past, but I just thought they were kidding, I didn't realize I actually was."

Julia huffed. "It's probably why I got the wrong idea. You were just trying to be friendly and I took it the wrong way. So, I will say, about last night…"

"I thought we were going to forget that happened?"

"Sure, but not until I apologize. I'm really sorry that I said all of that. I didn't mean to make things weird between us, and I'm not usually wrong about those things. I promise I won't ever bring it up again." Julia scuffed her foot along the carpet and stared down at it, awaiting a reply.

"I appreciate that. And Julia? If you actually do want to talk about this date, now or after, you can talk to me. I swear I'll listen and won't judge."

"It's fine. Not much to say at this point anyway." Julia turned quickly and hurried off to her office.

CHAPTER 5

Steph arrived a few minutes early the next morning, eager to exchange flirty banter with Julia once again and even to pry a little about how her date had went. Although she was kind of jealous that Julia even had a date, she knew it was an excuse to talk to her, but she told herself that's what friends were like. She stepped through the door of the break room to find Julia sitting on the counter and waiting for the coffee to perk.

"Hey! I kinda hoped I was going to run into you this morning. How was your night after?" Steph could feel her stomach roll as she asked the question.

"What? Oh, fine. Why do you care?" Julia shot back at her. "It's not like you actually want to know."

"Well, no. Probably not. But I said we could be friends, and this is what friends do, so I'm asking how things went."

"What would you like me to tell you? Everything? Spare no details kind of sharing, or were you just hoping I would say that it was alright, I had a nice meal and said goodnight?" Julia frowned and shook her head.

"I just hoped that you would want to talk to me about it at all, really. I didn't exactly have expectations of how much you would tell me or anything, and you are probably right. I don't want to know all the details if there are many to tell."

"She was fun. We had drinks, I invited her back to my place, we had a nice evening and then I sent her home. How does that work for you?"

Steph's stomach was in knots as she listened to Julia speak and she had to swallow hard to compose herself before she could reply. "That's nice. Does...does that mean that you are going to see her again?"

"Not likely."

"I'm not sure what happened between yesterday when we spoke and just now, but I guess you are mad at me again?" Steph furrowed her eyebrows in confusion.

"What do you mean? I apologized for what I said the other night, but I never said I wasn't still pissed that you dismissed me, that you want to pretend nothing was said or that you don't want to actually sit down and talk about it."

"Seriously? You're acting like a child." Steph took a breath and lowered her voice to just more than a whisper. "We talked about this a couple of times now. No matter how many times you bring it up, or what you say, it isn't going to change my answer. I'm sorry you got the wrong impression about how I feel about you. I'm sorry that we can't be more than friends, but I meant what I said. I do very much want us to be friends. I could use someone to relate to right now, and someone that knows what I am going through."

"So, you want to keep being my friend because we both sleep with women so that means I know what you are going through and can help?" Julia was getting increasingly angry as Steph spoke.

"What? Seriously, what's up with you this morning?"

"Nothing. Just another one-off date with someone that I'll never see again and today I go back to the search for someone that is worth more of my time."

"You know, maybe if you give someone a chance, they will surprise you. I mean, what can you really tell from just one date?"

"More than you would think. The last time I was in love, I knew it before the drinks even arrived at our table. We were together two years, but of course I can't keep it in my pants, so that didn't last. I've been single a long time. I know when it isn't worth it pretty quick."

"So, you are looking for a relationship then? Trying to settle down?"

"I'm just looking for some fun right now. You should be too, especially after all you went through with the breakup with Nicole." Julia rolled her eyes.

"Maybe I will then. You seem to be so gung-ho about this dating website, maybe I should be creating a profile of my own. It's not like it is safe to hit the bar to meet people right now." As much as she hated conspiracy theories, Steph was starting to believe Julia's assessment that the killer was purposely finding his victims at The Closet and it was the only local gay club.

"You should. I don't see what could be stopping you. You should hook up with as many girls as you like, and I will do the same." Julia slid off the counter, grabbed her mug from behind Steph and filled it from the carafe.

Steph held out her mug for Julia to fill but was left holding the empty cup as Julia slammed it back on the machine and marched out of the room. "I guess I deserved that," She muttered under her breath before filling her mug and making her way back to her office.

If she thought her morning couldn't get any worse,

Steph arrived back to her desk to be immediately greeted by an email from Nicole.

To: Steph Underwood
From: Nicole O'Brien
Subject: Mortgage

Steph,
I know you don't really want to talk to me right now, but I need to make sure that you are pushing the paperwork to have my name removed from the mortgage on the house. I need it off my credit so I can buy my own place to live. Please let me know what the holdup is on this.

Nic

Steph sighed, a lump forming in her throat to go along with the one that was already sitting uncomfortably in her stomach after her conversation with Julia. She had forgotten all about calling the bank to try to make the change to the information on the house with the distraction of her recent promotion and dealing with whatever was happening between her and Julia.

She knew that it was going to be almost impossible to get the bank to agree to remove Nicole from the mortgage and that she wasn't going to be able to get it refinanced without a co-applicant and she had been dreading the phone call to her parents to ask for their help. She only made small talk with them and rarely saw her family since she and Nicole had moved in together four years ago. She certainly had never asked them for help of any kind. More than anything, she was dreading coming up with an explanation as to why she was now going to buy Nicole's house and not have a roommate after all these years.

Beads of sweat formed on Steph's forehead as she racked her brain for reasons and excuses to give her parents that wouldn't make them suspicious. The last thing she needed to deal with on top of the breakup and the extra work was her extremely religious parents finding out about her sexual preferences.

It wasn't that her parents had pulled away from her, it was quite the opposite. Steph never saw eye to eye with her father, a man that she was too much like for them to really understand each other but he loved her, she knew that was true. Her mother had never been much of a parental figure, more a woman who treated her daughter as the best friend she never had. Steph figured that must have been because she was the youngest as she didn't treat her sisters the same way.

Steph just wanted to be able to live her life without their judgement, so when she moved in with Nicole, she cut off most communication with them, unless it was necessary. For the first time in almost six months, it was necessary, and Steph was dreading dialing the phone. She decided to delay the inevitable by first calling the bank to see what her options really were.

"Hello, I'm looking to speak to someone about the possibility of getting a mortgage." Steph nervously tapped her fingers on the desk as she spoke.

The voice on the other end of the line was overly chipper for 9AM, "Do you bank with us currently?"

"I do. In fact, I am already a co-signer on a mortgage through your bank. I am looking into the possibility of being the sole name on that loan."

"Well, we couldn't just take someone off the loan, you will have to get a new loan. Do you know who you dealt with for the first mortgage?"

"I don't remember his name." Steph was usually much more prepared when she was making calls like this and if it had been for a story, she would have had several stacks of paper in front of her with every detail.

"Okay, your name?"

"Stephanie Underwood."

The voice on the end of the line was quiet and Steph could hear the clicking of the keyboard as the woman searched through the computer for the information. "Just bear with me for a minute while I figure out who you need to talk to."

"Sure, sure. Take your time." Steph fiddled with the paperclips on her desk and scrolled through her emails as she waited.

"Okay. So, you have been dealing with Robert. He is actually free right now, so I'll transfer you in to speak to him."

"Great. Thanks."

"Robert speaking. How can I help you?"

"Good morning. I am wondering if it would be possible for me to get approved for a mortgage." Steph patiently answered a number of his questions about her finances, her current mortgage on the house with Nicole and the length of mortgage she was looking for going forward.

"Okay, unfortunately Miss Underwood it looks like you will still need a co-signer if you want to purchase the home. Even with your newly increased income with the size of down payment you are able to provide we will need a second person to sign for the loan."

She thanked Robert and hung up with a sigh. After almost an hour of answering his questions, Steph was still at square one and was not going to have any choice but to ask her father to co-sign.

Steph dialed the number quickly and held her breath as she waited for an answer. "Mom, hi. How are things going?"

"The same as always. Is something wrong?" Her mother replied through static on the line.

"Not wrong, really, no. I was hoping that we could get together for a chat. I need to ask you and dad about something, and I would rather not do it over the phone." Steph lied. She would most definitely rather do it on the phone, but she knew they would ask less questions and be more likely to say yes if they had to look her in the eye when she asked.

"Well, I suppose we could come out to the city on the weekend. Then again, you know where we live and could just come home for dinner on Sunday?"

Steph tried to hold her fake smile so her mother would believe she sounded happy about the idea, "I suppose I could do that. In fact, that sounds lovely. Supper at 6?"

"I suppose we could make that work. We will see you then." Her mother hung up the phone without a good-bye.

CHAPTER 6

Steph overslept on Sunday morning and had to rush to get ready to make the two-hour drive to her parents' house in the suburbs. She was hoping to have the difficult conversation about money with them before supper so she could skip the meal altogether if it didn't go well.

Steph's hands were shaking as she drove, and she cranked up the music to try to occupy her mind. The local radio station DJ was droning on about some upcoming children's event in the park and she found her thoughts drifting to Julia. It started with a professional wondering of whether Steph would send her to cover the event they were talking about and then drifted to more concern that she was making a mistake on the personal side of their relationship.

She shook her head trying to push away the thoughts rolling around inside it. No matter what, she knew that she was making the right decision about Julia. They could only be friends and the only way that she was going to stop having the regret was to start dating. She was a little nervous about the idea of using a dating website but spent the rest of the drive convincing herself to sign up when she got home that night.

Steph took a deep breath as she turned off the ignition

of the car in her parent's driveway. She had a lot of anxiety about going home to a place where she felt it wasn't okay to be herself. Steph had been pretending to be whatever she thought they wanted and expected of her from the first moment she realized she was gay and the way they were in their religion would never allow her mom and dad to think that was okay.

Steph had learned many coping mechanisms over the years to calm herself down and put on a smile before having to face her parents. She took a couple of deep breaths, dug her nails deep into her thigh and reminded herself that she put on this mask for many years while still living under their roof. Although it was harder now to have to put it back on for short periods of time rather than live wearing it, she could get through this one evening if it meant her life would continue on with the only change being no Nicole in it.

Steph was still a little upset about the breakup and to have to talk about buying the house and not be able to explain how much pain she was experiencing with the people who were supposed to love her the most was unthinkable. Her mother had always treated her like she was her best friend to confide in, but Steph had never once confided back, and she wanted nothing more than to be able to do so now. She wasn't close with her oldest sister, Sherri, they were too far apart in age, and although they had been close when they were young, she and her sister, Jane, had drifted apart after middle school and Jane had moved across the country the moment she graduated.

Steph slowly made her way up the steps of the front porch and tapped on the door before entering. "Hello! Mom, Dad! I made it." She cringed at the cross that hung in the front porch and the picture of the Virgin Mary that held the mirror in the hallway.

Steph felt the colour drain from her face as her mother came down the stairs with a scowl. She swallowed hard and forced a smile. "Hey Mom, it's nice to see you."

"I thought you would have been here earlier. Supper is almost ready, and I just woke your father from his nap." She absentmindedly wiped her hands in her apron that read 'God is Love.' "Come on in then. I'll be in the kitchen."

Steph slammed the side of the foot against the back of her sneaker and pulled it free before using her toes to remove the other. She kept running the conversation over in her head, what she would say and how she expected her parents to react to her request. It wasn't like she was asking them for money, but it felt like she was. Her mother was leaning over the oven when she rounded the corner into the kitchen, and she could hear her father's footfalls coming down the back staircase.

"Hey, Stephy! It's been a long time since you have made the effort to come out and see us," He said, slapping his hand down on her shoulder.

"Work just keeps me so busy, I guess. You guys don't exactly come and visit me either." Steph crossed her arms over her chest. She was more relieved that they stayed away, really. They had only visited twice since she had moved in with Nicole and that had been enough time for her to never want to listen to her mother's condescending comments about the art on the walls and how she needed to bring God into her home.

"Well, we didn't want to intrude on your roommate's space. Did your mother say she moved out? Finally found herself a nice boy, I suppose."

"Yes. She did move out. And she is offering to sell me the house. I looked into it, but I would need someone to co-sign if I wanted to buy. It's the best deal I am going to get if I ever want to buy a place in the city. She is offering to sell it for what is currently left owing on the mortgage where I have been paying into it for the last five years." Steph gasped for breath, realizing that she had rambled her full conversation without an inhale.

"That's nice, Stephy. I think this could be a really good opportunity for you to become more stable. I'm sure I would be able to co-sign on that mortgage for you. Then we will have a place to stay if we want to come down to the city." Her father smiled, not missing a beat. "But, I really wish you would be like your friend and find a nice fellow to settle down with. Are you seeing anyone now?"

Steph was in shock. She had been prepared to make a dozen arguments about why they should help, not for her father to agree and then talk about her house like they were going to use it for weekend getaways. "No, not seeing anyone. I'm focused on my career and now that I'm the Chief Editor, I have a lot more work to worry about." The words fell from her lips without even thinking. Steph had told the lie that she wasn't dating for so long that she didn't know how else to answer the inquiries anymore.

"Well, now that it's settled you can make an appointment for us at the bank for early this week and we can get this all taken care of right away."

"Okay guys, supper is ready. Steph, would you mind setting the table? I'm just going to grab the bread from the oven, and I will be right in." Her mother said as she grabbed the oven mitts to get the baking sheet.

They finally sat around the table and Steph fell into the familiar routine of holding hands with her parents as her mother gave a lengthy moment of reflection in the quiet before spending another five offering her thanks to God for the meal.

"You know, rub-a-dub-dub thanks for the grub would work just as well and dinner wouldn't be cold by the time you finished," Steph joked. Her father shot her a look and she blushed in embarrassment. Steph tended to forget how important the blessing of food was to her mother.

Dinner seemed to go on forever as Steph listened to her mother prattle on about how the vegetables were doing in her garden this year and how she wished Steph would make more time to visit with them and the rest of the family.

It was quiet for a few minutes when her mother dropped her fork on her plate and started to smile. "Stephy, do you remember Diana from my church group?"

"Kinda. She is the one with the four kids that recently came back to the group after a divorce?"

"You know, we didn't make her leave and that divorce was all her husband's fault. She would never have gone through with it, being a good Christian woman and all."

"Of course not, because good Christians can't wind up in bad relationships."

Her mother scowled but pulled her smile back to continue, "Anyway, her son Joe is living in North Beach now. He's about your age and she was telling me that he recently broke up with his long-time girlfriend. If you wanted, I'm sure I could arrange for you to meet him."

"That's okay, Mom, really. I'm so busy with work that I honestly don't have time for dating." Steph pushed the food around on her plate.

"But he is a good Christian boy, goes to church every Sunday and helps with the Men's Auxiliary. And he is a successful dentist." She said almost in a sing-song. "And, Diana showed me a picture and I think he is really cute!"

"Thanks, but no thanks. I really don't need you to set me up." Steph gritted her teeth, trying to stay as calm as possible, despite how badly she wanted to blurt out that she didn't want to be set up with a man. Maybe if her mom knew a nice single girl that was a cute dentist?

"Okay, but promise me that you will go to church more?"

"I'll try, Mom, but I work a lot of Sundays."

It was starting to get dark by the time she cleared the dishes from in front of her parents and loaded up the dishwasher.

"Well, I suppose I should be hitting the road. It's getting late and I have an early start again tomorrow. I have to meet with that new employee I told you about. Is Tuesday okay for the meeting with the bank, Dad?" Steph inquired as she shoved her feet down into her still tied sneakers in the porch.

"Tuesday will be fine. Just let me know what time and I will be there. And Steph, I really wish you wouldn't do that to your shoes. Sneakers are expensive and you will just ruin them." He ran his finger and thumb along the scruff on his chin as he spoke.

"It's okay, Dad. I buy them cheap just for that reason." Steph smiled and gave him a quick hug before turning to her mother. "Thanks again for supper, Mom. I really appreciate it. And I promise I will try to visit more often now that I won't be constantly chasing down a story." She hugged her mother and tried not to slam the door as she headed to her car.

Steph immediately felt a weight lift from her shoulders as she left her parent's house. It was the same weight she always felt lifted when she was no longer in her childhood home and no longer had to try to pretend to be someone or something that she was not; straight. She knew how her parents felt about 'alternative lifestyles' and she didn't think she was ever going to be ready to have them out of her life completely, so she planned to always keep them in the dark.

Steph thought a lot about how she felt hiding her sexuality as she drove back to North Beach. She had wanted to be the kind of person that could shout it from the rooftops and feel great just being herself, but she knew that it would turn her life upside down if people found out and she didn't want to deal with that.

Steph knew a boy in her high school that had come out in his first year of university and in some ways she kind of envied him. He had been truthful about who he was and although she heard stories of how badly his family had reacted at first, they were all very close now and he could be happy in a way that Steph never imagined feeling. But she also didn't know anything different than her own experience and it was too late for her to try to change anything now. She would just have to go on dealing with the heaviness of lying to her parents, the struggle of trying not to get too close to the people she worked with and the terror that someone who already knew would accidently let her secret out.

She could live without all the fear of having her parents meet any of her friends, on purpose or accidentally, but she still didn't want to have to deal with the backlash of what would happen should they know the truth. It would be far worse than having to deal with the constant questions about finding a nice guy and why she wasn't married.

Steph tucked her shoulder length dirty blonde hair behind her ear and turned up the music to try to drown out her thoughts. She was more than halfway home and wanted to get her mind to relax before she arrived so she could sleep. She flicked the radio station to the oldies channel and hummed along with the best of the sixties.

CHAPTER 7

Steph picked out her favourite pantsuit for her Monday morning meeting with Kerri Walters, the new photojournalist who would be arriving for her first day. She had decided that she would partner her with another reporter for the first couple of weeks so she could get her feet wet. She was planning to ask Julia to volunteer so she could press her for details about how their new staffer was doing.

As she waited, Steph found her thoughts drifting back to the first time she had laid eyes on Julia. She was sitting in her office, minding her own business, when Julia sauntered in and started rambling about whatever story she was working on.

"I'm sorry, have we met?" Steph stared at her, confused.

"No, I don't suppose we have. I'm Julia Demendo, the new junior reporter? I was told to come and give you an update on my story to see if you wanted to hold the issue, or if you want to wait until tomorrow to run it."

"Oh! Hi, sorry. I guess I was just so wrapped up in this piece giving the local take on the hanging of Saddam Hussein. I forgot Jamie told me you were coming."

Julia sat on the edge of Steph's desk and crossed her legs as she peered over to check out what Steph was looking at. "Oh, yeah. That is a big one," She commented as she leaned forward, almost throwing her cleavage in Steph's face.

Steph blushed and tried to avert her eyes. She pushed her chair back from the desk and folded her arms across her chest to try to act natural. "So, what is this great story that you want me to hold space in the paper for?"

Julia grinned and jumped off the desk, "Well, I have a source that says the city has spent half of the roads budget on streets that the mayor and councillors live on, and that is why we are dealing with so many pothole issues on Main."

"Hmm, that would be a big get. How credible is this source?" Steph felt the blood return to her body as she contemplated the political ramifications of the story.

"Very."

"Well, then I guess we will be finding you a few columns. Let me know when it's ready."

"Cool, yeah, cool. I totally will." Julia almost skipped out of the office and down the hall.

Steph just sat there for a minute after she left with a stupid grin on her face that she always had when she thought someone was cute, or at least that is what Nicole told her. She could feel the flush in her cheeks and already a little anticipation of their next interaction.

Steph shook her head, bringing herself back to reality and walked aimlessly down the hall to clear her thoughts.

Steph was impressed when Kerri arrived ten minutes early for the day. Steph was standing in the doorway of the lunchroom, watching Julia make coffee and waiting for a chance to get herself a cup when Kerri walked up to the front desk.

"Hi Kerri! Nice to see you like to be punctual. How about we start off with a tour of the office? Most people are already here, and it would be a great chance for an introduction." Steph smiled, trying to hide how nervous she was. "You can put your things in the office at the end of the hall. That is where you will be working." She gestured toward an open door a few feet away.

"Sounds great." Kerri slowly made her way down the hall to the office.

"New girl is kinda cute!" Julia elbowed Steph in the ribs, teasing.

"Oh Lord, are you getting ideas? She has barely had time to catch her breath in this city. Don't you get enough dates that you wouldn't have to chase someone you work with?" Steph shot back.

Julia laughed, "Okay, no need to get all green-eyed-monster, darlin'. I was just saying. She is definitely part of *the family*."

"Jesus, you think everyone is gay, don't you?" Steph whispered as she crossed her arms over her chest.

"Not everyone, just the ones that are. And there are a higher-than-normal number in this business, so it is probably a safe bet."

"You've also changed your tune since we spoke last week. Not pissed at me anymore?"

"Yeah, well, I decided to let it go and do what I said I would do; be friends."

Julia shrugged as they watched Kerri return from her new office. She raised her eyebrows knowingly at Steph as Kerri shyly smiled at them and stuffed her hands into her pockets. They stood awkwardly near the front desk for a few minutes just looking at each other before anyone spoke.

"So, I suppose I should get to work or something." Julia shuffled off down the hall before Kerri reached the desk.

"I guess we should get the tour underway." Steph gestured for Kerri to take the hallway to her right and followed behind, introducing her to a number of editors in the offices on the way to the bullpen of the main newsroom where a dozen junior reporters were seated in cubicles.

Julia looked up from her computer when they entered, "Hey! You again!" She chuckled, extending her hand for Kerri to shake. "I had a good feeling about you when you came in for your interview," she half flirted, holding onto Kerri's hand just a moment longer than was comfortable.

"Yeah. It's nice to see you again." Kerri blushed. "I'm really looking forward to getting to work with all of you." She slipped her hand away from Julia quickly before walking further into the bullpen to introduce herself to some of the other junior reporters.

"Told you she played for our team," Julia ribbed Steph.

"Shut up, would you?" Steph whispered. "I should be giving you a warning for inappropriate workplace activity, knowing what I know. I'll pretend for the moment that I don't...and let that slide."

"Thanks, boss." Julia winked.

"That isn't any more appropriate," Steph scoffed folding her arms across her chest.

"So, I can't flirt with the new hire, I can't wink at the boss. Any more rules that I should know about? I wouldn't want to get myself into any trouble."

"Ha ha," Steph replied sarcastically. "You know the rules. You just love to push the boundaries, from what I can tell. I'm just saying that you should watch yourself."

"Yeah, yeah. I will. But you know what they say, at least a third of all relationships start at work." Julia grinned.

"Well, I'm surprised. I didn't think you were the relationship kind of girl. Seems like you have a new person on your arm every other week."

"Not because I'm not willing to make it last longer, guess I just haven't found anyone worth settling down for. Besides, it's hard to meet someone who is who they claim to be online and with the hours we work, it's hard to meet people any other way."

"Do you even give them a chance? Good lord, you go out once or twice and you toss them aside. I wouldn't even have had time to decide if I was really interested by that point."

"Yeah you would. You're just a serial monogamist that can't stand the idea of being alone so one date turns in to a long-term relationship, whether it should or not."

"How dare you make that presumption? You barely know me, and you certainly don't know enough about my dating history to think that. I've gone on lots of dates that didn't turn into relationships."

"Only because the other person wasn't interested. I might not know everything about you, but I know your type. I bet from the minute that Nicole left you immediately started looking for a new relationship."

"I did nothing of the sort," Steph scoffed.

"That just makes me wonder if you are still hoping she will change her mind."

"Not at all. She was right. All of the reasons that she gave me for leaving were right on the money. I have no delusions that she is going to come crawling back and I don't foresee me chasing after her either."

"Good to know. I should probably grab a coffee and get back to work. The crime page won't write itself. You should also catch up with the newbie." Julia gestured toward the bullpen where Kerri seemed to be getting a little overwhelmed with the number of introductions.

"You're right. You should get back to work." Steph pulled her shoulders back and brushed a strand of hair from her face before marching down the hall to Kerri's side.

"Kerri, I see you are getting acquainted with all of the folks around here! Why don't we continue the tour and then you can get settled into your office?"

Kerri released a breath she didn't realize she had been holding and nodded. "That sounds great. I can't wait to get started on my first story in the big city."

"Well, I was thinking that you might want to work with one of the other reporters for the first little while. Just so that you have someone to guide you around, show you the ropes. I know things can be a little more fast paced here than what you are used to."

"I'd be alright with that. Does it matter who? I mean, do I get to choose? Should it be one of the senior staffers?" Kerri rambled.

"You can certainly decide who you want to work with, and no, it doesn't have to be a senior reporter. It's almost time for the morning break. Most people hang out in the staff room around this time, so this is probably a good chance for you to ask someone."

"Perfect. I'll get right on that." Kerri shook Steph's hand, "Thanks again for this opportunity."

"It's well deserved. We will meet again in a couple of days to see how things are going."

Steph hovered outside the break room and watched as Julia approached Kerri and struck up a conversation. She could see that Julia was flirting and felt a lump forming in her stomach. Steph shook off the feeling when she realized that Kerri was oblivious to the way Julia was acting but then had a sudden moment of panic that the feeling was not fear that she was going to have to reprimand her friend, but a touch of jealousy.

Once she was sure Kerri had asked to tag along with Julia, Steph headed back to her office to try to get back to work. She stared at the computer screen for close to an hour without even reading the words, mulling over the idea that she was feeling jealous. She was trying to convince herself that it had nothing to do with anything that she might be feeling for Julia, but a jealousy that she was able to be so open with her sexuality and so confident to just casually flirt with someone in public.

Just after lunch Julia popped her head through Steph's open door, tapping on it as she leaned her head around the corner. "Hey, so I'm dragging Kerri along with me to the murder thing this afternoon. It's about damn time I don't have to take my own photos and notes at the same time." Julia winked.

"It's a big story and you should have asked to have a photographer assigned before now anyway." Steph sighed and shook her head. "I'm glad you are going to get her started."

"Of course. It should be a bit of fun. And I'll make sure to take her for a welcome to town drink after work too." Julia smiled coyly.

***

It was getting close to four o'clock when Julia finally poked her head back into Steph's office to announce their return. "She did great. A real professional, although I don't know that I expected any less. I should be ready to head out within the hour."

"I wasn't worried about how she was going to do. I just didn't want her getting lost or feeling intimidated here in the city for the first little while. I've been there and it can really burst your confidence to show up late because you got lost." Steph brushed her ponytail over her shoulder. "I suppose you want her on this story until you see it through?"

"Damn right I do. It cuts my work in half and I have a feeling this is going to turn out to be a much bigger story than the cops are willing to let us believe right now." Julia glanced at her notepad.

"What makes you say that?"

"Well, for starters there have been three women killed that I think I can connect back to the lesbian bar on Main Street, The Closet, whether the police are willing to admit it yet or not. I have a feeling this is a serial killer situation, and they don't want to create a panic just yet."

"I hate to say it, but that is a pretty good instinct. Just don't go writing your speculation into the story, got it?" Steph pointed a finger at Julia as though she was scolding a child.

"You got it boss. Something in my gut says this is going to be a wild ride and I wanna take a certain photographer along for it."

"I hope you only mean that in a professional sense." Steph scowled.

"For now. Let's see how it goes, shall we?" Julia chuckled and turned to leave, "I'll see you tomorrow."

"That you will. Now, run along and get that story filed."

CHAPTER 8

Julia arrived early Wednesday morning, already grumbling when Steph passed her in the hallway on the way to the lunchroom. It wasn't unusual for Julia to get to the office around the same time Steph did, but Steph had also arrived early that morning for a meeting with the overnight staff. She thought about just leaving her to grumble but was only a few steps down the hall when she turned around and went back to check in on Julia.

"Well, you aren't your usual chipper morning self today, and you are even earlier than usual. Something wrong?" Steph leaned as casually as she could against the doorframe of the lunchroom, arms folded across her chest.

"Yeah, bad breakfast date. But I'm sure you don't want to hear about it." Julia drank down the remaining coffee in her cup and turned to refill it.

Steph gritted her teeth and tried to force a smile, "I didn't realize you were seeing someone. Does she know how big a flirt you are?"

"I'm not really seeing someone. It was just a first date with someone I had been talking to online and, as usual, they weren't at all who they pretended to be. It's just so frustrating." Julia slammed her cup down on the counter, spilling a little of the freshly poured coffee. "Damn it. This day is just off to the best start."

Steph had already grabbed a handful of paper towel to help with the mess before Julia could even locate the roll. "Maybe breakfast dates aren't the best way to start your day?" She smiled and shook her head as she mopped up the coffee. "Besides, I thought you were making a play for the new girl..." Her voice trailed off as she felt a lump of jealousy grow in her stomach.

"No worries there. She is so not interested in me."

"So, you were wrong about her after all? Maybe your gaydar isn't as good as you think it is?" Steph smiled, feeling a little better that Kerri and Julia wouldn't be an item.

"No, no. Nothing like that. She is definitely into women, just really hung up on someone else so even if I did stand a chance, it wouldn't be going anywhere, and I'm not interested in a one-night stand with someone that I have to work with all the time. If I was going to date someone at work, it would be because I thought there was a future. For now, I'm just going to stick to my dating site and see if Mrs. Right just appears, not that I'm holding out any hope that it will happen."

"Maybe I should actually give that a try," Steph thought out loud, "Then again, after hearing about your bad morning, maybe that is the totally wrong way to go. I just wish it was easier to meet people, you know? It can be so hard to tell if a woman is just being friendly or if she is flirting. It's not like I can just ask without constantly outing myself either, and what if it isn't flirting and I make a total fool of myself? I don't remember this ever being so hard."

"It's not hard if you aren't afraid to tell people. There are also some pretty distinct differences between nice and flirting. For example, I'm generally flirting with you. Now you don't have to ask." Julia smiled coyly.

"Yeah, yeah. But that's just you being you. It doesn't mean anything." The lump in Steph's stomach made its way into her throat. "What is this dating site you are using? Maybe I will sign up."

Julia swallowed hard. "Maybe you shouldn't. This is the third bad date I have been on in the last week. I'm going on another tonight, if that goes any better then I will suggest you sign up."

"You have another date tonight? That's insane! Are you really that hard up that you are making multiple dates for the same day?" Steph was getting increasingly irritated at the idea of Julia dating so much. "Don't you think that feels a little desperate?"

Julia stood with her mouth agape, staring at Steph. "I am certainly not desperate! Dating was easier before I was afraid to go to the club and I could meet a real live person and decide if I liked them. Now, I feel like everyone pretends to be one thing online, and then when you actually meet them, they are completely different. I know you clearly think I'm just some sort of player, but that isn't me at all. I would love to find someone that I want to be with for the long term, someone that I could see myself settling down with and having a real relationship. It just seems like every time I find someone that might fit that bill, they aren't interested for one reason or another."

"Well, I guess I will get the rundown on date number two tomorrow. I should get to work. This paper isn't going to plan itself." Steph bit her lower lip and headed toward the door, "you ever think you are just misreading the signs?" She muttered as she walked away.

"What was that?" Julia yelled after her, but Steph just

ignored her and continued on to her office, closing the door behind herself.

Steph flopped into her desk chair and exhaled as though she had been holding her breath for her entire conversation with Julia. She hadn't meant to suggest that if the flirting between them was more than just a game she would like that; it just came out. Steph wasn't even sure if Julia had heard the comment and wanted her to clarify or if she actually didn't hear what she said.

She barely had time to ponder it when there was a knock at the door. Steph swallowed hard as it swung open and Julia bounced into the room and planted herself in front of the desk, slamming her palms down on the edge.

"You make some offhanded statement like that and then just walk away and close the door on me? What are you trying to say?" Julia paused, but didn't really expect a response. "I'm tired of going around in circles with you. You can't make me feel guilty about dating, you have no right to judge me for how many people I go out with and you can't tell me that I don't know how to read the signs that someone is interested. Especially, *especially*, when you are talking about yourself and I can only believe what you are telling me."

"Would you keep your voice down? I shouldn't have said it. I'm sorry. I really can't — whether I want to or not — be anything more than your friend. We have been over this time and time again. I'm not going to do it again, especially not here," Steph quipped, "You should get back to work. Early press conference, right?"

"Yeah. I guess I should. I won't bring it up again as long as you don't." Julia turned and stormed out of the office, slamming the door behind her.

Steph could feel tears welling up in her eyes and she

swallowed hard, trying to push them down. She wasn't sure why she was so upset; she was never one to be emotional over almost anything. The tears quickly turned to anger, and she opened her internet browser to search for the dating website Julia had been using.

Steph quickly filled out the form, giving almost every detail about her life, but not her real last name. She wouldn't disclose that until she found someone she liked, just in case someone else she worked with was on the site and saw her profile. She also refused to put up a photo. She knew that was going to lower the number of people who might contact her, but she just couldn't be too careful. It only took her about ten minutes to finish the profile and she immediately started to scroll through potential matches. Steph wasn't sure if she was doing it out of spite, or some extreme effort to make herself believe that she didn't care about Julia.

There were several pages of potential matches that Steph thought seemed at least a little interesting. She quickly minimized the window when she came upon Nicole's profile. Steph could at least take some solace in the fact that Nicole having a profile meant that she didn't actually leave her for someone else, but it did cement even more that all the secretive things she had done to keep her sexuality quiet really did cause the breakup.

With morbid curiosity she opened the screen again and clicked on Nicole's picture. She knew that photo well. She had taken it the summer before. They had gone on a weekend trip to the country, rented a cabin and spent three solid days away from anyone they knew. It had been a freeing experience for Steph who felt like she could be herself for the first time. She even let Nicole hold her hand as they walked through the streets of the small town nearby. Steph had thought about proposing on that week-end, but something told her she was only doing it to make Nicole happy, and looking back, she really was.

Nicole had used the picture as her first profile photo when they signed up for Facebook a week later and Steph had printed a wallet size that she carried around with her. She pulled the wallet from her back pocket and took out the picture, staring at it for only a moment before throwing it in the trash bin beside her desk. She couldn't help herself and had to scroll through Nicole's profile.

Steph shook her head and went back to the list of other profiles. She wasn't really sold on the idea of a date with a stranger, but she had to start somewhere. 32 years old and single was bad enough when 'single' just meant she was keeping her relationship a secret, it was really depressing when she was actually alone.

This was the first time she had been alone in more than a decade. She had been in a couple of long-term relation-ships prior to Nicole, one right after the other and she had barely said the words 'it's over' in the last one when she found herself in bed with Nicole which turned into the last five years of her life. Truth be told, she wasn't sure she really knew how to be alone.

Steph clicked on one of the profiles of a girl she thought was kind of cute but couldn't bring herself to send a mes-sage. It suddenly occurred to her that she could wind up going out with someone that Julia had already dated and all of those had apparently been horrible dates. And how would Julia feel if that happened?

Steph didn't want to create any more tension between them. She really did want to be friends, if nothing else, and it was hard enough with the tension she already felt when they were together. She took a deep breath and decided it didn't matter if she picked someone Julia had already seen, there wouldn't be any jealousy because Julia had already rejected them.

Steph mustered all her courage to send a message when she saw that she had received a message on her own profile. She shuddered with excitement and anticipation to see who had been brave enough to send her a message without a picture.

Hey! I guess you are new on here, but your profile seems interesting and I would love to get to know you better.

Steph started grinning, she had forgotten the thrill of a first interaction with someone new. It didn't hurt her confidence to know that she had only just put up her profile and she had already received a message. She took a minute to look at the woman's profile before replying. "Dawn Mendoza, 29, PR. Recently out of a long-term relationship, loves hiking and watching all things gay on television," Steph read aloud. "Seems like someone my speed."

Hey! What did you have in mind?

Steph tapped her fingers against the keyboard, anxiously awaiting a reply. She wasn't sure how quickly any of this worked, but she didn't want to seem like she was ignoring this girl and she didn't know the protocol on if you could wait all day to reply like an email, or if you should respond right away, like a text message. She barely had time to ponder it when she received another message.

Want to get a drink and go from there? We can go to The Closet tonight?

Steph had never set foot in the local gay bar and she wasn't about to start now, especially with girls being killed. Plus, what if she saw someone she knew there? It was bad enough that Jamie and Julia had figured it out, she didn't need anyone else knowing right now. She was going to have to take the chance that she would run into people at a less gay place.

With everything happening at that bar, I would rather pick a different place, somewhere a little more quiet too, so we can talk. How about La Bistro?

Steph chewed at her fingers, waiting for a reply.

La Bistro sounds great. How is 7?

7 works great. It's a date.

Steph quickly closed the internet browser and quietly squealed to herself in excitement. She was going on a date for the first time in years and she wasn't sure if she was terrified or happy about it. Whatever it was, she had all day to figure it out, and a ton of work to do so she could get there on time.

CHAPTER 9

Steph sent the final version of the Thursday paper to the printer at 6:30 that evening and rushed home to change her clothes. She needed to shake the grime of the day with a fresh outfit before meeting Dawn at the restaurant. Steph grabbed her favourite t-shirt, tossed on a pair of jeans that had been sitting on her bedroom floor for over a week and grabbed her keys, pausing to take a quick glance in the mirror and a deep breath before leaving the house.

She pulled up in front of the restaurant at 6:59 and checked her hair again in the rear-view mirror before heading in. Steph was looking through the large front window for her date when she ran directly into Julia who was on the way out.

"Don't tell me, another failed date for you tonight?"

"Haha, no." Julia lied. "I live upstairs, so I ordered takeout. I do that most nights. What brings you here? Hot date already?"

"Umm…" Steph paused. "Sort of?" She squeaked.

"Well, you aren't wasting any time. I told you that you couldn't be alone. Just don't rent the U-haul just yet, okay?"

"So funny," Steph replied in a sarcastic tone that seemed to be reserved for her conversations with Julia. "I haven't even met her yet. But I think I see her waiting and you are going to make me late."

"Okay, I'll get out of your way. Have fun!" Julia called out after her.

Steph walked as confidently as she could to the table where her date was sitting, sipping a glass of wine.

Steph cleared her throat, "Dawn?" The girl nodded. "Shall I sit?"

Dawn stood from her chair and gestured at the place across from her. "Yes, of course, yes, sit."

Steph flagged down the waitress and adjusted her chair awkwardly. "So, do you do this much?"

"Drink on a Wednesday? I try not to." Dawn giggled uncomfortably. "I don't date much either. I was with someone for a few years and she was really only my second girlfriend 'cause I stayed with the first one for five years when it should have been five months. Sorry, that's too much information so fast."

"Oh, I know that story. We all have that someone that should have been a best friend and we let it become more and then it was too hard to get out of it and you didn't want to lose the friend."

Dawn grinned, "Exactly. It's a weird line. How about you?"

"This is the first date I have been on in more than…five years? I just got out of a relationship so I should warn you that I don't know if I'm looking for anything serious."

"Well, how about we just take a few minutes to decide if we even like each other before we start talking about how serious a relationship we are looking for."

Steph laughed. "Sorry, you are absolutely right. I also want to apologize in advance if I ask too many questions. It's the hazards of being a journalist. Sometimes I can make people feel like they are being interviewed when I first meet them."

"It's okay, I'm in public relations. I'm used to feeling like I'm being interrogated." Dawn chuckled.

"So you get it then? The hours, the people we have to deal with and be nice to, even if we don't want to."

"Oh, for sure. And there is nothing worse than dealing with the insanity and drama all day and then having to face more of it at home." Dawn shook her head.

"So, I take it your job was part of the reason for your most recent break up?" Steph asked.

"Part of it. And I guess now is as good a time as any to tell you, but I don't really tell people I'm gay. In my line of work, you have to keep as much of your life private as you can. Is that a problem for you?"

"If I'm being completely honest, I don't broadcast my life either. There are a few people who know, but for the most part, I keep it to myself. Not even my family knows." Steph bowed her head, embarrassed at the admission.

"Really? That doesn't seem like any way to live. How do you keep it from the closest people to you?"

"Maybe I should have started with the fact that we aren't really that close. They live a couple of hours away and I don't see them often. Christmas, funerals, you know, the usual." Steph noticed she was wringing her hands on the table and quickly tucked them in her lap. "Plus, they are really religious people and as long as I keep it quiet, they will still want to be a part of my life…Shoot. Over-share?"

"A little. My family knows. My close friends too, but I don't like to tell my co-workers or the media people I deal with. I don't know how I would manage without my support system." Dawn smiled. "Well, how about we change the subject? Tell me more about you."

"Well, where to start. I was born and raised here in North Beach and I have never really left. I stayed here for school and everything, so I guess I'm not all that interesting in that regard."

"On the contrary. I think it is really interesting that you have always lived here. I would never have been able to stay in my hometown. I like my privacy too much to have stayed around the people I grew up with. Plus, I had this crazy girl that I dated in high school who stayed at home and the idea of running into her at the grocery store or the post office makes my stomach roll." Dawn laughed.

"Oh, we all have one of those," Steph said, "the girl who made you do things you can't ever imagine doing again and just knew exactly how to push your buttons so you felt like you spent more time fighting about breaking up than being in a relationship to start with."

Dawn fidgeted with the napkin on her lap. "This one was more like a straight girl that just really liked the attention and yes, knew exactly how to push all my buttons to make me feel like I was losing my mind all the time."

Steph laughed. "It's been a long time since I talked about my crazy. Nicole...my recent ex, hated it when I would talk about my past relationships. Made me make it a rule that we didn't do that when we first started dating."

"That's a bit of a weird rule. Do you think it was more about her?"

"Oh, it was definitely more about her. She didn't want to talk about the girl she left to be with me."

"Oh, do I sense a scandal?" Dawn chuckled.

"I don't know about that. But I wasn't really upset that she wanted to leave the past in the past. Might be the best thing I can do now, too."

"Or you might never heal from it if you don't talk about it at all. And trust me, having doubts about how a past relationship ended and no one to talk to about it can really screw up the next one."

"I suppose that is what your friends are for though, don't really want to dump all your past relationship crap on someone that you have just started dating. That could really screw it up too." Steph stared at Dawn, waiting for a reaction.

"There is that too. So, I guess that eliminates a ton of the conversation starters I had for tonight." Dawn paused as the waitress stopped beside them, notepad in hand.

"Well, ladies, what can I get for you?" The waitress smiled and tapped her pen against the notepad.

Steph glanced down at the menu in front of her. "Well, I never veer from my usual, so once again I have no idea why I'm even looking at this."

Dawn passed her menu back to the waitress. "I'm probably just going to have a drink."

Steph looked up, startled. "Oh. I didn't realize it was that kind of a date. I'll just have a beer."

"I'll have one too." Dawn waited for the waitress to walk away before speaking again. "It's not 'that kind of date' at all, I just figure start with a drink and if it is going well, order some food in a bit. I'm sorry if I gave you the impression I was looking for a quick out."

"It's cool. Like I said earlier, I haven't done this in a long time, so I guess I just don't know the protocol these days. I mean, I had never even been on a dating website until last week. I must seem very naïve to you." Steph bowed her head.

"Not really, no. You seem like someone who has been

out of the game for a while, that's all. So, tell me something else about yourself."

"Like what? I feel like I am my job, so there isn't much to tell."

"Okay...well, this might sound weird, but tell me your favourite childhood memory." Dawn nodded at the waitress as she placed the beers down in front of the two women.

"That is a little weird. My favourite childhood memory?" Steph rubbed her thumb and index finger over her chin. "I had a fairly average childhood I guess, but I really loved the moments when I would get to go camping. My nan had this little trailer that she would take me to for a weekend or a week at a time. Sometimes it would be parked by her brother's cottage and other times it would be on the ocean with a bunch of other family cabins. We would play cards and pick mussels from the ocean when the wind would blow the right way and bring the seaweed on shore. There were old comic books in the drawers of the bunk beds from when my dad was a kid that gave me my first love of them. I still love camping too and I go as often as I can, which is usually when Jamie, my old boss, forced me to take vacation time. Guess I will have to force myself to take the time now." Steph's thoughts momentarily drifted to her new responsibilities and she wondered how Jamie balanced everything so easily before remembering she was on a date and should keep the conversation going. She forced a smile, "How about you?"

"The slide. The way the metal of the slide would burn my ass and thighs because my shorts would pull up as I went down. Kids these days have no idea. Plastic slides. Blah. Where is the challenge in that? If it isn't an injury waiting to happen or a complete death trap, what is the point of a playground?" Dawn laughed.

Steph suddenly swallowed hard as the door of La Bistro opened and Kerri Walters took a seat at the bar. Her heart rate increased as she looked at the woman sitting across from her whose expression told Steph she realized something had changed about the evening.

"Something wrong? You look like you are ready to bolt on me. You didn't like the slide?"

"No, no. My new hire just walked in." Steph swallowed hard.

"Oh, do you want to go say hi, or invite her over?"

"It's okay. I don't think she has noticed me, so I'll just leave it. What were we talking about?"

Steph watched Kerri at the bar for a minute, not really listening to what Dawn was saying and became even more distracted when she saw Julia enter and sit with her. Steph's mind raced. She suddenly realized that she wouldn't be able to handle those two dating and being all lovey-dovey around the office. The last thing Steph needed was Julia all over some girl at work, or worse, having her create an awkward situation by going out with her a couple of times and them breaking up. It was enough for Steph to have to hear about the women Julia was dating and the hearts she was breaking, she didn't need to experience it first-hand. However, she had paired them up for the Closet Murders assignment so if they were dating, it was her own fault.

"And when I realized that I was too soft hearted to ask the really hard questions or be first on an accident scene, I decided to switch gears and go into PR." Dawn finished her story and her beer and waited for Steph to acknowledge the quiet. "Are you even on this date anymore? I don't think you have heard a word I have said since your co-worker came in."

"I'm sorry. I guess I am distracted." Steph's gaze continued to focus on Julia and Kerri at the bar who had now been joined by a third woman who Julia seemed to be introducing herself to. "Tell me more about your work?"

"It's really not that interesting," Dawn continued to speak but Steph's attention was focused only on the three women sitting at the bar.

"That's cool. Sounds like it keeps you really busy."

"Yeah. Hey, Steph, I think we should call this a night. I mean, I was having a great time, but now you seem more interested in everyone and everything else that is going on and I don't want to ruin the fact that this was going well up until now."

"I'm sorry. I really am. I don't know why my attention is all over the place all of a sudden," Steph lied as she tried to read the body language and the lips of the women at the bar.

"It's okay. But I am going to go." Dawn stood from the table and Steph stood with her.

"Are you sure? I really was having a nice time with you tonight."

"I'm sure. Besides, it's after 8 and I have some work to catch up on for tomorrow."

"Okay. Well, it was really nice meeting you and getting to know you a little. I hope we can do this again sometime," Steph grinned as the words fell out of her mouth.

"I think we could arrange that." Dawn handed Steph her business card, "Call me. We can set something up for dinner this time."

Steph barely had the card in her pocket when the brunette she didn't know at the bar with Kerri and Julia suddenly ran out the door with Kerri following close behind her. Julia continued to sit at the bar and Steph watched her exchange pleasantries with Dawn as she approached the door.

"As if this night didn't just get awkward enough," Steph muttered to herself as they chatted a few feet in front of her. She waited a few minutes for Dawn to leave before adjusting her shirt and making her way to the bar to pay for their drinks. "Twice in one night, are you keeping this place in business?" Steph tried to play it cool as she approached Julia.

"Well, I'm certainly trying. How did it go?" Julia nodded her head toward the table where Steph had been seated with Dawn.

"Okay, I guess. We seemed to be hitting it off and she did ask me to call." Steph chewed on her lower lip and waited to see how Julia would react, almost hoping to see some sort of hurt or disappointment in her face.

"I'm really surprised that she is back on the horse so fast. You know she was dating the first victim in the Closet Murders, don't you?"

"Wait, she was what? Like for a long time, or…"

"Just for a couple of weeks, but I think that would mess me up more than it seems to have her. She didn't mention anything about it?"

"No, nothing. I did make some comment about Nicole teaching me not to talk about people I had been with in the past, so we didn't get into our past dating life. She probably didn't want to share that with a reporter she just met either. Probably afraid of all the questions."

"Could be, but I doubt it. It was one of the first things she told me when we went out last week. It's probably really raw and she is either trying to forget about it, or you know, she is a sociopath who doesn't care. I mean, they did only go out a couple of times, so it isn't that weird that she is seeing other people."

"Are you just saying this to freak me out?" Steph crossed her arms over her chest and glared at Julia.

"No. Not at all. I just figured she told you. Although, you weren't paying much attention to her at all once Kerri and I came in."

"You two seem to be getting pretty close. Anything I should know about?" Steph cleared her throat, "From an HR perspective, I mean."

"Nah, she is totally head over heels for the girl she chased out of here. You don't have to worry your pretty little head about anything between me and Kerri as long as Summer is in the picture."

"That's good." Steph caught herself, "I mean, I would hate to have to worry about a ton of paperwork on top of the craziness of this week with the serial murders interrupting our printing schedule and taking over the front page."

"I'm sure that's your problem with it." Julia rolled her eyes.

"Anyway, I should get home. Tomorrow is going to be a long day." Steph pulled on her jacket and turned to the door. "See you in the morning."

"Yeah, see you then."

CHAPTER 10

Steph could feel goosebumps forming on the back of her neck and a slight tremble of her hand as she walked into the Observer offices the next morning. She had no idea what kind of reaction to expect from Julia after the conversation they had at La Bistro the night before. She decided to skip coffee in the break room and head straight to her office instead of risking accidently running into her.

Steph still wasn't sure if Julia was saying those things just to mess with her, or if it was true. She also hadn't really taken the time to process that Julia said she had gone out with Dawn the week before. Part of her wanted to run into Julia so she could ask if they were friends or if they had been on a date. It might be hard to just throw into conversation, but she wasn't sure how she felt about calling Dawn again if she had already slept with Julia.

Steph shook her head, trying to push the image of the two of them together from her mind. Whatever had happened between them was none of her business anyway and it was only going to make her stomach more upset to continue to think about it. She was just able to focus on something else when Julia tapped and opened the door to her office.

"Hey. Sorry if I freaked you out last night. I just

thought you should have all the facts. You gonna see her again?" Julia held onto the doorknob, only stepping half-way into the room as she spoke.

"It's okay, I haven't decided if I'm going to call her or not yet, but it isn't anything to do with whether or not she once dated someone who is dead." Steph paused, wanting to ask the one burning question on her mind, but decided against it.

Julia fully entered the room and closed the door behind her. She puffed up her chest, "then it must be about me." She winked.

"Actually, for once, you are kinda right, but not in the way that you think," Steph blurted and stood from her chair.

"Really now? Well, how is it about me if it isn't about you leading on that poor girl because you would rather be with me?"

"You said you went out with her last week?"

"Yeah. We had a drink together and I realized right away that she wasn't for me. Is that the problem? You think that if I go out with someone it automatically means that I have had sex with them?"

"Well, I mean, that is the way that it seems."

"Wow, just...wow. I had no idea that you thought I was such a huge slut." Julia's face flushed red with anger. "I'll have you know that despite your terrible opinion of me, I don't have sex with everyone that buys me a drink. In fact, I'm pretty selective about who I invite into my apartment, never mind my bed."

"Geez, I'm sorry, okay? You are the one that gives the world the impression that you sleep with a half a dozen women in the run of a week. I don't know why you are so upset that I believed your posturing."

"I'm not posturing. And I have never tried to give any-one the impression that I'm a whore. Just that I could be if I wanted to. So, to answer your question, no, I didn't have sex with Dawn. I didn't even kiss her."

Steph felt a little weight lift from her shoulders, a re-lief that she wasn't sure was about the fact that the sec-ond date she was thinking about going on wasn't with someone that had already slept with Julia, or if it was more about finding out that Julia hadn't gotten around as much as she had previously thought. "I said I was sorry. I shouldn't have judged you like that. I guess I just believed what I wanted to believe."

"I guess you did. Can we just drop it now, please?" Julia turned toward the door. "So why don't you just go ahead and give your new girlfriend a call. If you don't see her tonight you won't be moved in together by the end of the month and we can't have that."

"Maybe I will." Steph flopped back into her chair and glared at Julia.

"Fine. I hope you have a wonderful life together." Ju-lia left the office, closing the door just a little too hard.

Steph just sat in silence looking at the door for several minutes after Julia left. She struggled to process what had happened for them to be fighting like this all the time. It felt like she was a teenager again, fighting with her first girlfriend, except without all the making out that fol-lowed. She felt like every time she saw Julia she was just putting her foot in her mouth over and over again.

"I just have to stop making so damn many assump-tions about her," Steph muttered to herself. "We were just starting to become friends and then Nicole left and now it is just a weird mess of I don't know what is happening and all we seem to do is wind up mad at each other for some reason or another. Maybe she is right, maybe I just need to focus on finding someone to be in my life and maybe that will make all of this stop."

Steph took out her wallet, pulled out Dawn's card, and slapped it down on the desk in front of her phone. "Deep breath and just dial the number. You call dozens of people every day. Just call and see if she wants to go out again. No big deal." She could feel the palms of her hands start to sweat at the idea of just pushing a few buttons but still lifted the receiver and began to dial.

The ringing started on the line and Steph suddenly couldn't think of a single thing to say as a woman's voice answered, "Ah, yes, hi." She panicked trying to think of what she should say next.

"How can I help you?" the voice said after a short pause.

Steph felt further panic when she realized she didn't know her last name and the business card had fallen under the desk. "I'm calling to speak with, ah, Dawn?"

"That would be me. How can I help you?" Dawn chirped through the phone.

"It's Steph. From last night."

"Oh, hey Steph. I was just thinking about you." There was a slight change in her voice as she went from business professional to more casual and alluring.

"Really? I mean, I'm sorry if this is too soon, or too forward, but I was having a good time with you last night before I got so distracted and I first wanted to apologize for how I acted when some of my staff came into the bar."

"It's okay. I was having a good time too. In fact, I was thinking about checking out a movie tonight. Final Destination 3 is out now, or if you want to be really corny, we could see that one, Date Movie?"

"Oh, you want me to go with you?" Steph choked out.

"Of course. Why would I bring it up if I wasn't going to ask you to come?" Dawn giggled.

"Well, I haven't seen the first two Final Destination movies, so…"

"What? How have you not seen Final Destination? It's got Devon Sawa and Kerr Smith and Amanda Detmer. I mean, even I had a little crush on Devon Sawa when I was a kid. How could you not go see it?"

"I was a poor student when that one came out, so I didn't go to a lot of movies. And to be honest, I don't really watch many movies these days either. I'm too busy to commit to two hours on one thing that isn't work."

"So, maybe a movie is a stupid suggestion? Do you want to do something else?"

"No, no. I'd love to see a movie with you. Just might be a good idea to stick with something that isn't a sequel."

"Ha ha ha, then you probably don't want to see Date Movie either. It is just a parody of a bunch of rom coms that have been released over the last couple of years."

"Like what? I was forced to watch a bunch of those over the last four or five years, I might actually enjoy that." Steph perked up. For once the fact that Nicole had constantly brought home stupid romance movies might be good for something.

"Ummm, I think it is mostly Bridget Jones and that Greek Wedding one. I know there are others, but I'm not sure what ones."

"Well, I have seen both of those, so we could totally go to Date Movie if you want."

"Awesome. I guess it's a date. Do you want to meet at the theatre, or…?"

"No. I'll pick you up. What time is the movie?"

"Let me just look it up."

"It's okay. I have the morning edition right here." Steph flipped to the entertainment section of the paper and ran her finger down the column to the theatre listings. "Looks like we have a choice of a 7pm showing or a 9:30."

"Why don't we do seven in case we want to call it an early night with work in the morning."

"Yeah, okay. We can totally do seven."

"It also leaves some time to hang out after if we aren't too tired."

Steph's grin grew wider at the suggestion. "Sounds great, I'll pick you up?"

"How about I pick you up? I live across town from the theatre so it would take you way out of the way to come get me and have to take me home afterward."

"Okay, sure. It's 12 Country Road, the big burgundy two storey on your right near the top of the one-way street."

"Great. I'll be there at 6:30? I wanna make sure we have time to get snacks."

"Okay. I'll see you then."

"Bye."

Steph waited to hear the click of Dawn hanging up her end of the phone before placing the receiver back in the cradle and dancing around her office like an excited schoolgirl over the prospect of a second date.

Steph pulled herself together and rushed to answer a knock at her office door. "Kerri! What can I do for you? I know we haven't had a chance to chat since you started, but it's great that you and Julia have been working so well together." Steph could feel a surge of jealousy at the amount of time they had been spending together, but continued to smile as she gestured for Kerri to enter and closed the door behind them. "Take a seat. Tell me, how has the first week been treating you?"

Kerri took a seat in the same chair she had been sitting in just a few short weeks ago when Steph had first offered her the job at the Observer. "Things are going great from my perspective as well. Julia is a great reporter and has been wonderful about showing me around the city and helping me get adjusted to all the new programs and procedures."

Steph couldn't help but cringe a little as she wondered exactly what procedures Julia had been teaching her outside of the office. "Wonderful. I knew you would make a good team. And how are you adjusting to city life?"

"It's good. Julia has been helping with that as well, taking me to a couple of local places. I also have an old friend in town that I have been spending time with, so I think I'm really going to like it here."

"So, what can I do for you today?" Steph took a seat behind the desk, crossing her legs and shifting a stack of paperwork to better see Kerri.

"I was hoping that it would be okay if I left the office for a couple of hours. I have everything well in hand here and I wanted to take some time to snap a few stock photos for several stories that I have on the backburner."

"I think that is a wonderful idea. Plus, it is a beautiful day and lord knows I would be trying to find a way out of this office if I wasn't drowning in paperwork." Steph smiled. Finally, a photographer with some initiative to get ahead of the game. For most journalists there was no way to ever get ahead, unless you wanted to write obituaries for people who weren't already dead.

"That's great!" Kerri jumped from the chair and tossed her camera bag over her head. "Thanks, Steph. I will have my phone with me so you can reach me if I am needed. Otherwise, I will be back in a little while."

Steph waited for the door to the office to close before going back to her celebration. Looking forward to her date with Dawn would help push Julia from her mind, she was sure of it. She shifted the stack of paperwork back in front of her and decided to dive in to make sure she wasn't late for the movie.

CHAPTER 11

At 6:15 the stack of paperwork in front of Steph seemed bigger than it was that morning when she started but she knew she needed to leave the office if she was going to get home in time to change and not make Dawn wait. It was only a couple of minutes to walk down the road to get home, but she needed to pick out an outfit and freshen up a little before Dawn arrived.

Steph checked the clock as she entered the porch at home, just five minutes later but she had no more than taken off her jacket when there was a knock on the door. She checked herself in the mirror in the hall before opening the door to reveal Dawn, casually dressed in a tight v-neck shirt, flared jeans and a leather jacket with just enough makeup to show she was wearing it at all and that she had made an effort for the evening.

"I'm sorry, I'm not quite ready yet. I just got in the door from work. Make yourself at home. I'll only be a few minutes," Steph shouted back as she headed to her room to change. "There's an open bottle of wine in the fridge and juice and all those things if you would like something to drink."

"I'm good," Dawn shouted back down the hall.

Steph rushed around her room, trying to quickly pick

out an outfit that would complement what Dawn was wearing but not match. She finally decided on the t-shirt she had picked up in New York a few years back when Nicole had taken her to see Rent for her birthday, a black suit jacket and the darkest jeans she had in her drawer. She took a minute to compose herself and catch her breath before putting on a smile and heading back into the living room to face Dawn.

"Well, are you ready to go?" Dawn smiled as she saw Steph appear in the hallway.

"I am. Shall we?" Steph grabbed her keys and gestured to the door.

Dawn stopped in the doorway and blushed as she turned toward Steph, putting on her shoes behind her. "Just one thing first."

"What's that?" Steph took a step forward toward the door as Dawn placed a quick kiss on her lips. "W-what was that for?" Steph stammered.

"Just thought we should get it out of the way. Now we can both relax and enjoy the evening, and no one has to wonder if it is going to happen or not." Dawn grabbed her by the hand and led her into the driveway and to her car.

***

The pair were still laughing when they walked back to the movie theatre parking lot, hand in hand. It was the first time that Steph had been so calm about holding another woman's hand in public. She wasn't even thinking about it until she saw Nicole approaching with a couple of her former friends.

Steph stopped dead in her tracks and let her fingers go limp, breaking the hand hold without shaking Dawn away. She just stared for a minute across the parking lot as Nicole and the other girls got closer.

"Are you okay? You look like you have seen a ghost." Dawn followed Steph's eyes to try to see what she was looking at. "Do you know them?"

"Yeah, you could say that. One of them is my ex and the other two are a couple that we used to be very close with until she up and left me after five years with barely an explanation."

"Well then. Should we get out of here quickly or flaunt how great this evening is going in front of them before calmly getting in the car?"

"How about wait and see if they want to speak to me? I'm sorry this is going to be another weird ending to a date, and we have only been out twice."

"It's okay. But it does look like one of them is coming this way." Dawn grabbed Steph's hand and pulled her a few steps closer to the approaching woman.

Nicole stopped about six feet from the pair and waved once, sweeping her hand in front of her shoulder. "Hey. How have you been?"

"Pretty good. Your life must be pretty crazy with the whole serial killer thing happening."

"Yeah, lots of extra hours. I've been a cop for over a decade, and I have never seen anything like this. North Beach is a small city, so the first death was only the third homicide I ever dealt with. It's more than crazy and this guy…or girl is really escalating with almost a daily death toll at this point."

"I do miss getting the inside scoop from you. But, ah, was there some reason that you came over to talk to me?"

"I just wanted to say thanks. You know, for taking care of the whole mortgage thing so quickly and for leaving me alone after everything. The girls talk all the time about how they have exes that are still constantly trying to contact them and things. I guess it's because you moved on already." Nicole gestured at Dawn who was still gripping Steph's hand.

Steph glanced at the girl beside her, having almost forgotten she was there. "Oh, sorry. Nic, this is Dawn." She choked, "but we have only gone out a couple of times."

"That's cool. I'm glad you are getting back out there. And you seem like things have really changed." Nicole snorted, nodding toward their joined hands.

"I guess they have, a little. I told you it would be different once I got the promotion. I said things would change, it's not my fault that you didn't believe me." Steph could feel her anger building as she spoke, and she gritted her teeth to try to keep her voice low and calm.

"I'm glad it did. And it wasn't like that. It wasn't that I didn't believe you. It just wasn't enough. Anyway, we have been over all of this and I don't think this is the time or place to rehash it all. I just wanted to say hi, show you that it wasn't weird to run into each other. It's going to happen, and I thought it would be better to try to make it okay right away, rather than avoid each other."

"I'm sorry. I didn't mean to bring any of that up. How are things with the case, Detective?"

Nicole changed to her professional tone of voice, "As you know, we don't have any real leads as of yet. I can't really say anything more than you guys are getting at the press conferences. We have extra patrol cops on the streets every night and I have been spending more time as the lesbian bar than I ever did in my life…in a work capacity I mean. Just trying to keep people safe."

"Glad to hear it." Steph turned to Dawn, "Can we have a minute?"

Dawn nodded and released her grip on Steph's hand.

"Sure. I'll meet you at the car?"

Steph nodded in reply and watched as Dawn walked toward where they were parked before turning back to Nicole. "Make sure you are keeping yourself safe too, okay? We may not be together anymore, but I still care about you and want you to be okay. It was always scary to have you out on the front lines, but even more so with a killer on the loose."

"I know. I still care about you too and I'm really glad that I haven't seen you kicking around the bar since all this started." Nicole chuckled, "Not that you were ever much for trying to pick someone up at a bar."

"This is very true. Anyway, I shouldn't keep you with your friends waiting. You are probably going to miss your movie."

Nicole checked her watch, "Yeah, it's getting close to show time so I should go." She started to walk away before turning back quickly, "Hey Steph, tell Dawn she better take good care of you, or she will have me to deal with."

"Ha ha, so funny. Maybe one day we could wind up friends?"

"Yeah. One day."

Steph turned to walk toward the car, glancing back over her shoulder to watch as Nicole jogged back to where her friends were waiting.

***

Steph smiled at Dawn as she jumped into the passenger side of the car and quickly buckled her seat belt as Dawn put it in gear and started to drive away. Steph took a deep breath in as though she was about to speak but thought better of it and just continued to let the ride happen in silence.

"So, is it going to be weird like this every time we go out or…?" Dawn couldn't help but laugh a little.

"God, I hope not. To be honest, I was surprised that you even wanted to see me a second time after the way our first date ended." Steph just stared out the windshield as she spoke.

"But here we are, on a second date in just two days. I just feel so comfortable with you already. It's not something that I feel often."

"Boy, you just lay it all out there, don't you?" Steph finally looked over at Dawn who made eye contact as they came to a stop in Steph's driveway.

"I like to try to be as blunt as possible. It saves time with either one of us having to guess what the other one is thinking. I know most people don't work that way and it can really put some off, but it's just the way I need it to be." Dawn shrugged.

"I can appreciate that. I mean, I'm certainly no mind reader and I know not talking has created a lot of problems for me in the past."

"So, with that in mind, are you going to invite me in for a drink?"

Steph could feel her face get hot as she flushed at the suggestion. "Ah, sure. I mean, of course I am. Would you like to come in for a night cap?"

Dawn turned off the engine and got out of the car with only a smile in reply. She waited by the driver's side until Steph was out of the car and then followed a step behind her as she walked up the front step and unlocked the door.

"Do you mind if I use your washroom? The upsize soda might have been a bad choice," Dawn asked as the door opened.

Steph threw her keys on the small table in the entry

way of the house and kicked off her shoes. "No problem. It's down the hall on the right. You can't miss it."

Dawn nodded and quickly dashed down the hall as Steph made her way to the kitchen and threw open the refrigerator. "I have some white wine, juice, milk, water…" Steph shouted back at Dawn as she heard the door of the bathroom open and the sound of the fan cease. She opened the cupboard over the fridge, "It looks like I also have some vodka, maybe enough for a drink of gin and one of these little bottles of rye." Steph turned to find Dawn just a step behind her in the kitchen.

Dawn placed one hand around Steph's waist and slid the other under her chin, tipping it up into a gentle kiss. "I guess I'll have a glass of wine. Just a small one though, I still have to drive, and tomorrow is another workday."

Steph leaned into the kiss, feeling her face flush with a rush of adrenaline. She pulled back, looked into Dawn's eyes and licked her lips, tasting a hint of sweetness from the candy they had at the movie from Dawn's mouth. She wrapped her arms around Dawn's waist and pulled her closer, making them look like a couple of high school kids slow dancing. "This is nice. It feels strangely comfortable."

Dawn chuckled, "It does, doesn't it?" She brushed her fingers softly across Steph's cheek. "It's like we have done this a hundred times before. So cheesy, right?"

"Nah. I don't mind cheesy at all. I think it's cute." Steph blushed slightly and half smiled.

"I shouldn't have chosen a movie for tonight. I feel like we didn't get to talk at all." Dawn stepped back from the embrace and took a long sip from her glass of wine.

"I think we talked enough last night to make up for it, don't you?" Steph poured her own glass of wine and gestured for Dawn to take a seat on the couch. She picked up the stereo remote from the coffee table and clicked it on before sitting down next to her.

The stereo came blaring to life as Matchbox Twenty's 'Yourself or Someone Like You' album filled the room with sound. Steph blushed and grabbed the remote to quickly turn it down. "Sorry, they have a new album coming out soon, so I was feeling a bit of nostalgia for one my favourites from my university days. I didn't realize I had left it up so loud."

Dawn just laughed and shook her head. "I, for some reason, am not surprised that you are listening to a decade old album from the 90s alt rock era. I'd be less surprised if it was a real oldie."

Steph tipped her head, "Why do you say that?"

"The décor? Every poster in your room is classic rock or old movies." Dawn smiled.

"Ahh…when were you in my room?"

"I might have taken a peek when I went to the washroom. You know, you can tell a lot about a girl based on whether she makes her bed and what she leaves out on her nightstand."

Steph looked at her slack-jawed. "I don't know if I should be upset that you invaded my privacy or impressed that you were trying to 'figure me out.'"

"You can close your mouth, I didn't touch anything or even really go in. The door was open, so I just had a little look around from the hall. If I was going to invade your privacy I would have poked around in your top drawer, or the drawer of the nightstand. *That* is how you really find things out about a woman."

Steph blushed again. She had never dated anyone as bold as Dawn seemed to be. She was relieved that she had taken a minute to make the bed that morning, or at least throw up the covers and fix the pillows before she left the house. She was still trying to remember if she had put the laundry away when Dawn leaned in and softly placed her lips on the edge of her jaw.

"Now, where were we?" Dawn carried her lips down Steph's neck, gently kissing just below the jawbone, then slightly lower before pressing her lips to Steph's exposed collar bone.

Steph's mind flashed with the memory of the last time Nicole had come to the house and what had happened on that couch. She felt a lump form in her throat at the idea of someone else's hands on her in the same place. She pulled back suddenly, causing Dawn to almost fall into her lap and then jumped to her feet as Dawn recovered her balance.

"Whoa. Is everything okay?" Dawn exclaimed, regaining her composure.

"Yeah, but I think it's time to call it a night." Steph ran her palms down over the front of her jeans.

Dawn stood from the couch. "I'm sorry, did I do something wrong? I thought this was going well."

"It's not you. I just don't know if I'm ready for this yet." Steph started to pace the floor. "I feel like I might be leading you on here, so I think it is time for you to go and us to call it a night. I just need to slow this down a little."

"Okay. I understand. You are just a few months out of a big relationship. I wasn't really expecting anything here tonight. I just want to make sure you know that." Dawn turned and walked toward the front porch. She pulled her jacket from the rack and was about to leave but stopped before opening the door. "Hey Steph? Maybe call me tomorrow when things are a little more clear?"

"I will absolutely call you tomorrow." Steph put her hands in her pockets and watched as Dawn left and quietly closed the door behind her.

CHAPTER 12

Steph stretched her arms over her desk chair, leaning her chest against its back and typed feverishly as she answered a number of emails on her Observer computer. Friday had been overly slow, but Saturday started with a flourish as she decided to head into the office to check in with Julia on the status of the Closet Murders story when she turned on the television to discover they had found a victim alive the night before.

She was also trying to avoid answering the text message from Dawn that had been sitting on her phone since the night before. She had decided that she was going to act 'like a guy' and not call Dawn for a couple of days after their Thursday night date but she was having a hard time playing it cool. She had meant what she said, that she wasn't ready to jump into bed with someone, but she did enjoy Dawn's company and it was nice to have someone around that made her laugh again.

Steph sighed as she finished her reply to the last new email in her inbox and pulled out the chair she had been leaning on to take a seat behind the desk. She was about to close the email and head to the break room for a coffee when the computer dinged again. She huffed and pulled the program back up on the screen to find an email from Kerri Walters.

Steph,

Sorry to send you this on such short notice, but I was hoping I could change my hours, at least for the next couple of days. My friend was badly injured and is in the hospital in critical condition and I feel like I need to be here for her as much as possible, especially overnight so that she is not alone. I was scheduled to do the 9-5 this week, but I was hoping to switch to the afternoon? It should only be for this week and I promise I will still put forward the same effort and keep in touch with Julia to make sure I am at any of the press conferences she needs me for, even outside of those hours. Please let me know as soon as possible.

Sincerely,
Kerri

Steph didn't hesitate before clicking reply. She had watched Kerri work harder than any of the other staff over the past couple of weeks, almost as though she was trying to prove to the rest of the staff, and herself, that she belonged there.

Kerri,
You can certainly change your shifts around. Please let me know if there is anything else that you need. I'm sorry to hear about your friend and feel free to keep me updated on her condition and things going forward. Looking forward to seeing you back at the office tomorrow.

Steph

Steph closed the email and poked a pencil behind her ear before heading down the hall to the breakroom. She picked up the carafe from the perk and shook her head.

No coffee. She started the water in the sink to fill the pot. As she turned around to start the brew Julia appeared in the doorway.

"Hey," Julia said casually, leaning against the frame of the door.

"Hey. What brings you in today? Isn't this your day off? I just emailed you about the girl who was found alive last night," Steph rambled.

"Yeah, I got the press release this morning and decided to come in. Figured I would try to get a few more details for our website if nothing else."

"Well, good on you. Way to show some real initiative. By the way, you will be without a photographer for today and mornings for the rest of the week." Steph finished placing the coffee grounds in the top of the pot, closed the lid and pressed the start button.

"Really? Kerri changed her shift? Any idea why?" Julia stepped into the break room and grabbed a mug from the cupboard.

"She emailed me this morning, something about a friend that got hurt and is in the hospital. I didn't ask any questions. It didn't seem like it was any of my business."

"Right on. I hope that is all that it is. I mean, some of it might be about avoiding me." Julia bowed her head, staring into her empty cup.

"Why would she want to avoid you? I thought you guys were working well together and getting along great," Steph said, "Please tell me you didn't do something stupid and try to put the moves on her or something…"

Julia laughed loudly, "Put the moves on her," she continued to laugh, struggling to catch her breath.

"What's so funny about that?" Steph couldn't help but join in on Julia's infectious level of laughter.

Julia finally grabbed a deep breath and wiped tears from her face. "I don't think I have called it that since high school, that's all. But, yeah, I guess I did a little."

"Oh Jesus, what happened?"

"Are you asking as a friend...? Or as my boss?"

"Is both an answer?" Steph half smiled.

"I just wasn't sure how much detail you wanted me to go into. I didn't do anything that means you have to call HR or something, if that is what you are worried about."

"Well, I mean, I am a little, but more so than that, I'm worried about you. I've seen you flirting with her and looking for her attention ever since she got here. Like, the other night when I saw you both at La Bistro with that other girl. You were working so hard to keep her attention from that other woman that you might as well have peed on her leg."

"The night with Summer? I was just getting her going. Summer, I mean. I was getting a kick out of the fact that Kerri was loving the attention and Summer was getting more and more frustrated the longer I kept it up. Come to think of it, I probably took it too far that night too." Julia shook her head.

Steph swallowed the lump in her throat that was trying to stop her from asking again. "Well, so what happened then?"

"Well, first of all, you need to know that Kerri is completely head over heels in love with Summer and I think has been for close to a decade, but Summer is with someone else and it is just a lot for Kerri to deal with right now. They had a big fight and Kerri was going to spend last night alone so I asked her to join me for dinner and a Buffy the Vampire Slayer marathon."

"Sounds like a date to me. Did she think it was a date?"

Steph filled her mug, poured some coffee into Julia's, and took a seat at the table next to the counter.

Julia sat across from her, flopping her body into the chair so hard she almost spilled the hot liquid all over herself and the table. "Well, I accidentally called it a date when we made the plan, but I made it very clear when she got to La Bistro that I didn't actually think it was one, I just said the word. We had a few drinks with dinner, probably a few too many, but that was my fault because I didn't realize she was such a lightweight."

Steph fiddled with the cup in front of her, "Okay, so you got her drunk and then what?"

"Well, after dinner we went upstairs to my place to watch the show and have a couple more drinks. We decided to just watch some of our favourite episodes, so you know we had to start with the musical."

"Of course, you did. That or the season seven episode where we find out Willow's new girlfriend has a tongue ring." Steph blushed a little at the admission.

Julia chuckled. "Well, of course, but back on the ranch, things were going great. We were having an awesome time singing along and even mimicking some of the scenes and then we got to the end. The big finale, 76 bloody trombones and getting your kumbaya-ya's out and all that, and as the swell of the music happens and Buffy and Spike kiss, I leaned in and kissed her."

Steph just stared at Julia. "Well, that is definitely the moment to do it if you were going to. I'm not sure I want to ask this, but then what happened?"

Julia bowed her head, not really wanting to make eye contact with Steph for the rest of the story. "Well, we started making out on the couch a little, but it didn't get any further than that. She put a stop to it and started going on about how she was thinking about someone else while she was kissing me and it wasn't fair. It wasn't anything I didn't know, and I just took advantage of what seemed like a moment. I wanted to see where it would go, I didn't expect it to be anything more than what it was."

"So, she was upset that you kissed her?" Steph watched as she swirled the coffee in her cup.

"I didn't think so, not really. Just upset that she was fighting with Summer and even though they aren't together right now, I think she wants them to be and doesn't want to jeopardize that in any way. She grabbed her coat and left after that to call Summer and apologize about their fight."

"I can see how you think she is avoiding you. I don't think she would lie to me about it though. I'm pretty sure if Kerri says she wants the later shift to stay with a sick friend that is exactly why." Steph tried to reassure Julia. "You need to be more careful in the future though! The last thing you need to do is make things weird for yourself at work."

"It wasn't like I planned it! It just sort of happened. On that note, how are things with Dawn?" Julia asked.

"I don't know. I'm trying to keep things from moving too fast, you know?" Steph paused. "I mean, she is really nice, and I think we have a lot in common and everything, but I don't want to accidentally find myself in a relationship without realizing what is happening."

"Sounds like you have been there before."

"Sort of. Hindsight is 20/20. I didn't know it when it was happening, and I just don't want to find myself there again. We had two dates in two nights and then I avoided her last night and I think she wants to see me again tonight, but I don't know if I want to."

Julia swallowed the last of the coffee and turned the mug on its side, rolling it around the table under her hand. "So, do you think you want to see her again at all?"

"Yeah, I do." Steph looked Julia directly in the eyes. "I like that she just tells it like it is and there is no confusion about how she feels or what she is thinking. It's refreshing."

"What is that supposed to mean?" Julia stopped rolling the mug and turned it upright with a thud.

"Just what I said. I like that she doesn't want to play games." Steph sighed and shook her head. "I'm an idiot."

"Huh? Why would you be an idiot?" Julia quickly switched from growing anger to confusion.

"Because I'm the one playing games right now." Steph stood from the table and pulled out her cell phone. "She is being so real and here I am trying to play it all cool and not call for a couple of days, but I do want to talk to her, and I do want to see her again. Therefore, I'm an idiot. I have to go call her."

As Steph was about to leave the lunchroom, Julia's phone binged with an incoming email. Steph paused in the doorway, waiting to see if it was more news in the Closet Murder case. She watched as Julia's eyes raced over the words on the screen and a small grin crossed her face, the kind of expression only a journalist can make at news of someone's death.

"News conference at noon. They have another body. I'm going to call Kerri and just let her know in case she wants to be there."

"Sounds good to me. Keep me posted on how it is going and make sure you let someone know that the story is coming in the layout department so they can save some space." Steph turned and headed back down the hall to her office without waiting for a response.

Steph closed the door to the office and sat in the chair facing the desk with her back to the wall. It hadn't been that long ago that she was sitting in that very spot when Jamie had told her she was going to take over the big chair. The same day that Nicole had decided to walk out after five years together, the same day she realized that her whole life was about to change at once. She understood that she wasn't the same person that had once sat in that chair. She had become the person that belonged on the other side of the desk.

Steph pulled the desk phone closer and slowly dialed the number on the business card that was now taped under the receiver. It rang several times, and she tapped her fingers against the desk nervously as she waited to see if Dawn would answer.

A groggy voice finally spoke on the other end of the line, "Hello?"

"Oh god, I'm sorry, I woke you up. I didn't realize you would still be sleeping. I didn't even think about what time it was and I totally forgot that it was the weekend."

"That is too many words for this early, but it's okay I should be up now anyway. To what do I owe the pleasure?"

"I just came to the conclusion that I think I was kind of avoiding you, but I was just trying to slow things down a little. I wanted to call and tell you that I would like to see you again, but maybe, next weekend?"

"Yeah, for sure. I tell you what? Why don't I give you a call a little later, you know, when I am really awake and we can plan something?" Dawn replied through a yawn.

"Absolutely. I'll talk to you soon." Steph hung up the phone, leaned back in the chair, linked her fingers together behind her head and kicked her feet up onto the desk.

CHAPTER 13

The following Friday things were starting to slow down at the Observer as police had released information about a man hunt for Doug Peters in the Closet Murders case and there hadn't been any incidents since the body was found the Saturday before. Steph had spent most of the week compiling the stories and photos Julia and Kerri had submitted on the case to submit for a national award.

Steph was totally engrossed in reading the most recent article when she heard a knock at her door. She looked up at the clock to realize she had been reading for over an hour and it was time for her meeting with Julia. "Come in."

"Hey, I'm a couple of minutes early. Do you want me to wait?" Julia hovered in the doorway.

"No, no. Come on in. I was just putting a few things together to submit to the national journalism awards and that is part of why I asked you to meet with me today." Steph shuffled the papers in front of her and placed them in a folder before sliding them across the desk to Julia. "So, here are the articles that I have selected for submission. First of all, I want to say I'm really proud of the way you and Kerri have handled this story. You have made us first out of the gate on so many new details and have proved to me that you have really grown as a writer over the last year."

"Wow. It means a lot that you think that." Julia blushed. "Please forgive my embarrassment, I'm not used to people praising me like this. And it's really cool that you want to submit our stuff. I really had no idea when it all started that this was going to turn into such a huge story. Thanks for not pulling me off it in favour of someone more seasoned."

"Of course not. It was your story to cover and you didn't give me any reason to think that you couldn't handle it. In fact, what you actually gave me was a reason to promote you." Steph pulled open the drawer of her desk and pulled out several pieces of paper with the North Beach Observer masthead that had been carefully stapled together in the corner.

"I thought you were worried that giving me any kind of promotion this soon would look like favouritism where we are friends?"

"I changed my mind. You have more than proven that you deserve it, and I don't think anyone else in the office would deny that fact. At this point, I think it would look strange if I didn't offer you the raise 'cause you know that is really what the promotion is. Nothing is going to change about your day to day and I don't have an office for you or anything, but you deserve the title and the money that goes along with it." Steph slid the papers and a pen toward Julia.

"Should I worry about the details of this contract, or just go ahead and sign it?" Julia joked.

"You can take all the time you like, but just keep in mind that I'm meeting with Kerri in a couple of minutes, so I need to get you out of here." Steph tapped her pencil against the clock on her desk. "Time's a wasting." She smiled.

Julia quickly signed the contract and slid it back to Steph who placed it back in the top drawer of her desk before standing and extending her hand to Julia. "Congratulations Miss Senior Reporter. I can't wait to see what you are going to do next."

Julia shook her hand and headed for the door. "Thank you so much. Kerri was waiting in the hall when I knocked. You want me to send her in?"

"That would be great."

Julia exited the office and Steph could hear her speaking to Kerri in the hall for a brief moment before Kerri entered. "Hi Steph, you asked to see me?"

Steph chuckled at the nervousness in Kerri's voice. "Have a seat. It's all good stuff, I swear." Steph waited for Kerri to get settled before continuing. "I just wanted to tell you that we are submitting yours and Julia's collaborative articles on The Closet Murders for a national journalism award. It's a rare honour as we only select a couple of pieces a year for submission."

Steph watched as Kerri struggled to find the words to respond to the news. She smiled as she watched the look of shock as Kerri's jaw dropped and Steph could almost see the wheels turning as Kerri processed the information. After a minute or so, Steph decided to put the girl out of her misery.

"I know you have been dealing with some personal things since you started and I also see the commitment you have made to the job, despite those issues and I commend you for it. I want to assure you that we will do what we can to accommodate you going forward as well." Steph extended her hand for Kerri to shake.

"Thank you. I don't know what else to say. Things are hopefully going to be back to normal soon. I really appreciate everything you've done, and I am trying not to let my work suffer." Kerri accepted Steph's extended hand.

"Well, it certainly hasn't so far. Thank you for taking the time to meet with me. Now, get back to work."

Kerri rose from the chair and headed out in the hall, leaving the door open just enough that Steph could hear the excitement as Julia shared her news with Kerri and they both took a moment to celebrate their joint achievement. The phone on Steph's desk started to ring, startling her back into reality.

"Steph Underwood," She answered casually.

"Hey, cutie! I was just checking in to make sure we are still on for tonight?" Dawn's voice was soft and chipper on the other end of the line.

"Hey yourself. Did you think I had changed my mind since we last spoke?" Steph twisted the phone cord in her fingers, something she hadn't done since the last time Nicole had called her at the office.

"Well, since I hadn't heard from you at all since we made the date, I just figured I should give you a call and see. I mean, I don't know anything that could make you want to stay away from me for more than a week, but maybe I missed something," Dawn flirted.

"Nope. You are exactly right. There is nothing more that I want to do than to see you tonight." Steph grinned to herself, "I'm really looking forward to dinner. We said seven, right?"

"Seven it is. I'll see you then." Steph had barely put the receiver back on the hook when Julia burst through the door of the office. "Yes?"

"Sorry, I was just excited. We have it on very good authority that police have made an arrest in the Closet Murders. I just wanted to give you a heads up that Kerri is on the way to the station to see if she can get some shots of the officers bringing him in. I'm going to make a couple of calls and get this confirmed so we can get it up on the website right away. Should I call layout, or do you want to? Let them know to hold some space for this one."

"I'll make the call to layout. You just get the confirmation." Steph picked up the phone and dialed the extension to the layout department. "And Julia?"

"Yeah?"

"Great job, once again. I know I already swelled your head this morning, but I just have to say that you have been really impressive on this one."

Julia just stood, looking at Steph and grinning.

"What are you waiting for? You have calls to make, get to it!" Steph laughed as Julia turned and ran down the hall to the bullpen.

***

Steph left the office early to prepare for her date with Dawn. She had rushed to get ready the first couple of times they had gone out and she didn't want to be in the same boat for date three. She had just stepped out of the shower when her cell phone rang, which she knew had to mean it was work.

"Steph Underwood," She answered as casually as she could through her frustration that she might have to go back to the office.

"Steph, Julia. Everything is ready to go, just wanted to know if you wanted one last look before I send it off to layout. You weren't in your office or the lunchroom, so this seemed like the easiest way to find you."

"No, it's fine, I trust you. Besides, I left early today." Steph struggled to hold the phone between her face and her shoulder while picking out an outfit.

"Oh, sorry to bother you then. Big plans tonight or something? It's not like you to leave early."

"Sort of." Steph held a shirt up in front of herself, then tossed it aside to hold up another. "I'm going to dinner with Dawn," Steph blurted.

"Ah, I see. What is this date number three? Cause you know what that means, right? I'm betting she has some expectations about what is going to happen tonight."

"Isn't that something straight people say? C'mon Jules. I really don't think either one of us was thinking about it that way."

"It might be something straight people say, but it is also something I say. I don't go out with someone a third time unless I want it to get serious."

"Yeah, I've kinda noticed that about you. Two dates and they are out the door. But never mind any of that. I have to get ready, so I have to let you go. I'm sure the story is great. If you really want, you can have Matthew take a last look."

"Alright, will do. Have a nice time on your date," Julia choked a little on the words.

"I will," Steph said slowly before ending the call and going back to her stress over her outfit.

Steph finally landed on her khaki pants that were just a couple of sizes too big and a black long sleeve t-shirt that was tight in all the right places. She quickly fixed her hair before grabbing her keys and heading out to the restaurant.

***

Steph could see Dawn seated at a table near the window with a half-finished beer in her hand as she passed the front of La Bistro on her way to the door. She picked up the pace, almost jogging the rest of the way into the restaurant and to the table. "I'm sorry. Am I late?" Steph stood behind the chair facing the wall and pulled her keys and her phone from her pockets, tossing them next to her place setting.

"Not at all. I finished up early at work and thought I would just head down here and grab a drink while I waited. Are you out of breath?" Dawn grinned.

"I thought I was late," Steph bowed her head shyly and sat down. "I might have run the last 20 steps or so," she laughed.

They fell into a rhythm throughout dinner, like old friends that had a level of comfort between them from spending many dinners together. Conversation came easy and soon Steph found herself sharing things about her life that she had taken years to even tell Nicole, and some of her biggest insecurities.

Steph looked up as the waitress approached their table and realized they were the only people remaining in the restaurant. "Have we overstayed our welcome?" Steph smiled.

"I just wanted to let you know that this is last call." The waitress removed the remaining empty plates and glasses from the table in front of them.

"Well, in that case, I suppose we should get the bill and let you fine folks go home," Dawn said as she passed her empty glass to the waitress.

"Sure, separate or together?"

"Together." Steph piped up immediately and pulled

her wallet from her back pocket, passing the waitress a card. "I would like the receipt."

Dawn blushed slightly from across the table as the waitress walked back to the bar to process the payment. "You didn't have to do that, but thank you for dinner."

Steph suddenly thought about her conversation with Julia and started to ramble. "I mean, I just, I had a great time and I wanted it to be my treat. I don't have any expectations or anything from this, I just..."

Dawn cut her off, "I know. I wasn't thinking that you were buying me dinner with some sort of ulterior motive." She giggled. "I wouldn't be mad if you wanted to continue this elsewhere, though."

Steph smiled shyly, "I mean, I would be okay with that. It is getting kinda late though."

"Well, how about if I walk you home?" Dawn stood and put on her coat.

"I would like that." Steph stood and placed her items back in pocket of her khakis before taking her card and the receipt from the waitress and placing both in her wallet.

As they reached the door, Dawn took Steph by the hand and guided her down onto the sidewalk before interlocking their fingers and taking the first steps toward Steph's house.

CHAPTER 14

When they reached the door, Steph turned and just looked at Dawn for a moment who took her other hand and pulled her closer, pressing their hips together as they continued to stand on the front step. Steph could feel the heat from Dawn's body against her stomach and the downward pressure she was putting on her hands to keep them by her sides.

Dawn pulled Steph's hands under her unzipped jacket and behind her back and unlinked their fingers, leaving Steph holding her around the waist. Steph could feel the exposed flesh of Dawn's back where her shirt had slid up over her jeans. Steph's chest shook as her breathing increased from the warmth of Dawn's skin beneath her fingers. Dawn giggled as Steph rubbed her hand along her back, tickling just a little.

"So, are you going to invite me in, or are we just going to stand here looking at each other?"

Steph blushed and tried to pull her hand back, but Dawn grabbed it and held it in place. Steph took a deep breath as she leaned in and pressed her mouth to Dawn's, pulling the girl's body even closer to her own and using her other hand to balance herself against the doorframe. She pulled back, glancing around the neighbourhood to see if anyone had seen.

Dawn placed her fingers on Steph's chin to hold it in place. "Paranoid or something?"

"Or something. Would you like to come in?" Steph felt a rush of adrenaline as the words spilled from her mouth. Her hands trembled as she pulled the keys from her pocket and tried to force it into the lock on the door.

Steph tossed the keys on the small table by the door and turned toward Dawn who kicked her shoes to the side and wrapped her hands behind Steph's back, grasping onto her shoulder blades. She pulled her in so they were practically nose to nose and stared into her eyes.

Steph could feel the pressure of Dawn's fingertips as they gently gripped her back and she slipped her arms over her shoulders and leaned in, gently pressing her lips to the tip of Dawn's nose and then her cheek before finding her lips.

Steph wasn't sure she was making the right move, but her body needed this. She needed some sort of release that only the touch of another person could give her. She longed for how it was with Nicole, or the way that she had often imagined it would be with someone like Julia. She pulled out of the kiss, almost shutting it down, then and there, but changed her mind.

Steph looked into Dawn's eyes and she could see her plead with her to keep going, without ever saying a word. Steph kissed her again, hungrily, stopping only long enough to pull her shirt over her head and forced her down the hall toward the bed. She wasn't interested in romanticizing what was happening.

Steph removed the rest of Dawn's clothes quickly and threw her weight back onto the pillow as she ripped off her own shirt and unbuttoned her pants. She had never been one to rush the foreplay and get right to the point, but as much as she wanted this, she also wanted it to be over already. Her uncertainty about being with someone new was getting the better of her but she remembered what Julia had said about it, it's only new until it isn't, and you never learn if you don't try new things.

Steph went through the motions, kissing Dawn's neck and across her collar bone, listening for her reaction and focusing on the way her hands were stroking the back of Steph's own neck and shoulders. Steph slowly moved her lips down over Dawn's body, kissing her stomach and the top of her hip bone. Every move was so familiar, yet so different in every way.

Steph wanted to ask if she was making the right moves, if Dawn was okay, but she wasn't sure if she should speak or if that would ruin the mood. She ran her hands up Dawn's sides and across her stomach as she continued to make her way down her body. She pressed her lips to her thigh and finally heard a reaction from Dawn. Steph knew she was ready and moved to gently kiss the most tender part of her body, feeling the warmth and the wetness of it on her tongue.

Steph paused just long enough to feel Dawn squirm before flicking her tongue faster and faster. She gripped onto her thighs, trying to keep her body still from the writhing and contracting of her muscles until she finally shuddered, telling Steph she was done.

Despite it all, Steph couldn't help but smile proudly at herself for bringing her to the point so quickly. Now came the part that she was dreading. It had been a long time since Steph had felt the touch of someone other than Nicole and she was terrified that her nerves would hold her back from enjoying the moment. She also found her mind wandering to Julia and wondering what advice she would give her right now, but she shook the thought away and tried to focus on Dawn.

She tried to relax as she threw her body down on the pillow beside Dawn and waited to see what she would do. Steph could feel the hairs on her arms stand on end from the chill of the air in the room as she laid naked and still, waiting for Dawn to recover. She wasn't waiting long when Dawn groaned and turned to face her, stroking her fingertips over her bicep.

The goosebumps on Steph's flesh multiplied and her whole body shivered. She could already feel the excitement swelling within her as she tried to anticipate Dawn's touch. She closed her eyes as Dawn softly wrapped her mouth around one of her erect nipples and slowly sucked. She focused on the warmth of her mouth as she kissed her way down her body and repeated the steps that she had just taken.

Steph couldn't say she didn't enjoy the feeling and the newness of everything, but it was also throwing her off. Between that and the alcohol she had consumed that evening, she couldn't seem to shift her body enough to get Dawn to touch exactly the right spot that would make her reach orgasm. She only opened her eyes to glance at the clock beside her on the nightstand and after a few minutes, she decided just to fake it and let it end.

Steph couldn't remember the last time she had faked it, but she could tell she had done a good enough job to convince Dawn that she had completed the task. Steph kept her eyes shut as Dawn crawled up next to her and placed her head on her shoulder and her hand across her stomach. She felt a single tear fall over her cheek as she realized that this was the moment that she had actually accepted that she and Nicole were never getting back together, and it was really time to move on.

She pulled the blankets over herself, and Dawn slid up next to her. Steph's mind drifted to thoughts of what it would be like to feel Julia this close and whether she would feel differently if that was the person who was beside her right now. She wondered if she would have been less in a rush to just get it over with, or more inclined to hold on every second. Maybe nothing would have been different at all, it was still going to be her first time after Nicole. Steph sighed and closed her eyes.

***

Steph was still naked and covered only in the bedsheet when she rolled over to look at the clock the next morning. She could smell Dawn's shampoo on her pillowcase and feel the heat from her body beside her. She softly traced her fingertips along Dawn's spine, stirring the girl from her sleep.

"Good morning." Steph smiled as Dawn lifted her head slightly, just one eye open.

"Oh shit. I didn't mean to stay." Dawn pulled the blanket up over her body to cover her exposed flesh as she rolled over onto her back.

"It's okay. We just kinda fell asleep." Steph brushed the hair from Dawn's face and kissed her lightly before moving to sit on the edge of the bed. "I'm going to make some coffee, if you would like." Steph pulled a pair of shorts and a t-shirt from the drawer in her nightstand.

"Coffee sounds great. Let me just find my clothes and I'll be right out." Dawn laughed, glancing around the room to find her bra draped over the lamp and no signs the shirt she had on the night before.

Steph's hands were still trembling as she tried to fill the coffee carafe in the kitchen. She hadn't planned on anything that happened the night before and she was suddenly worried she had only taken things to the next level because of her conversation with Julia. If she was being honest with herself, she had thought about Julia almost the whole time she was with Dawn.

Steph turned back toward the living room and noticed a blue shirt hanging off the back of the couch. She shook her head, picked it up and started to take it to her room to Dawn when she noticed the girl coming toward her down the hallway, her jeans not buttoned and her arms crossed over her upper body, clothed only in her lacy bra. Steph couldn't help but stare at the little indents of muscle around her hips.

"I think you are looking for this?" Steph smiled, passing the shirt to Dawn and trying to avert her eyes.

"Are you playing shy now? I was wearing a lot less than this last night. I'm not offended if you look. In fact, I'm kind of flattered that you want to." Dawn took the shirt, but just threw it over her shoulder, wrapping her arms around Steph's waist and pulling her into a kiss. She slipped her fingers behind the button of Steph's shorts and ran her fingers along the flesh of her stomach and the edge of her underwear.

Steph pulled back quickly and almost ran into the kitchen. "Coffee is ready." She filled her cup and pulled herself up to sit on the counter as she handed Dawn an empty mug. "Sugar?" She asked as she reached into the cupboard beside her head and pulled out the canister.

"Black is just fine." Dawn filled her cup, glancing back and forth between the coffee maker and Steph. "Did I do something to make things weird this morning?"

"No, I, ahhh, I'm just feeling a little overwhelmed, I think. Last night was a big deal for me and I went into the evening telling myself that I wasn't ready and that I wasn't going to let anything like that happen and yet, here we are."

"I'm sorry. I didn't pressure you or anything, did I?" Dawn placed her hand on Steph's knee.

"No, nothing like that." She tentatively placed her hand over Dawn's. "I just promised myself that I would take this slow and I didn't do that. We have barely known each other two weeks and you just spent the night. I wanted to take some time and get to know you first. I wanted my friends to meet you and then take the next step."

Dawn laughed, "So, you just wanted to plan how this would happen but instead it just did and now you are freaking out. Does that about sum it up?"

"Yeah, I guess it does." Steph sighed. "I know that things are already really comfortable between us, but I also wanted to make sure we have that thing, you know?"

"That thing?" Dawn furrowed her brow.

"Yeah, that chemistry that makes us work as more than friends. I don't want to wind up jumping into a relationship only to find out that I screwed up what should have been an amazing friendship."

"Ah, yes. The classic 'do I like her like that, or is it just convenient that we both like women' thing," Dawn laughed. "I hope you can tell that I'm attracted to you in more than a friend way."

"Yeah, I got that, but attraction doesn't necessarily mean anything." Steph paused and checked her watch. "Oh shit. I hate to do this, but I have to go into the office for a bit."

"Okay, I'll get out of here." Dawn dropped her mug in the sink.

"No, no, there is no need for you to rush out the door. You can stay as long as you like. Just lock the door behind you if you leave before I get back."

CHAPTER 15

Steph put off seeing Dawn for the rest of the week-end and managed to avoid anything more than a short phone call all week. The next weekend, Dawn had a girl's trip planned with her friends, so Steph was off the hook once again. On Wednesday of the second week, Steph was working with her office door open for a change when she noticed someone dressed more formally than her report-ers walking down the hall.

Dawn flipped her hair over her shoulder as she strut-ted toward the office door in her pencil skirt and white blouse, with just one too many buttons left undone, and green high heels that matched her skirt perfectly. She tapped on the doorframe to announce her presence before closing the door and sitting across from Steph.

"So, let's talk about why you are avoiding me." Dawn crossed her legs and leaned back in the chair and Steph couldn't help but feel a little like she had just found her-self in the movie Basic Instinct. "I didn't wait around for you that morning after we slept together because it felt like you needed a little space and I let you put me off all last week, but I just need to know if you are trying to end things and just don't know how to say it, or if I still have a chance here."

Steph swallowed hard. "I really don't know how to answer that. I was having a lot of fun with you. I think we have a lot in common and that there is definitely some chemistry here."

"So, what is the problem?" Dawn sighed.

As if on cue there was a knock at the door, startling Steph back to reality. She looked at Dawn and shrugged before answering. "Come in."

"Oh, sorry, I didn't know you had someone in here," Julia stuttered uncharacteristically. "I thought we were supposed to meet about the court coverage this morning?"

Steph blushed, "We are. I won't be long. Can you give me a few minutes and I'll come find you when I'm ready?"

"Sure, sure, no problem. I'll just go get a coffee so find me in the break room when you are set." Julia mouthed sorry again before closing the door gently.

Dawn waited for the sound of footsteps to move away from the door before speaking. "Oh! I see. It actually isn't about me."

"What do you mean by that?" Steph scratched her head.

"I mean, you have a thing for her! I should have realized it the first time we went out. The second she was at the bar you almost forgot I was in the room, you just kept looking over at her and the two girls she was with. I can't believe I was so stupid, and I didn't see it."

"Wait, just wait a minute. You have this all wrong. Julia is just a friend, and I'm her boss, there is nothing more to it than that." Steph could feel her heart rate increase as she spoke.

"I can't say I really believe you. I'm not blind, I can see

the way you were looking at her just now and I'm going to be honest I don't know if I want to continue this if I'm the second choice. Can you be honest with me and yourself and tell me that isn't what is happening here? You are going out with me because you feel like you can't be with her?"

"First of all, I am with you. There is nothing happening with Julia, nothing. But isn't it a little soon for you to be worried about any of those things? We only went out a couple of times. You don't know me at all, and you are trying to tell me what I want and that I am going to make you feel like you are second best?" Steph composed herself quickly. "I'm sorry. I don't know why that upset me so much. What I mean to say is that no one is first or second choice or third or any other choice. I find you attractive and fun and I was trying to see where this could go but I felt like it was moving too fast, so I pulled back a little. I should have had a real conversation with you about that rather than just making the statement, but it seemed like I didn't know how to find the words when I was with you."

"I'm sorry, too. You're right and I'm projecting feelings from my last break up on you right now and that isn't fair. And it really isn't fair that I'm doing it at your place of work." Dawn looked down at her watch. "I'm going to be late for work, so let me start this whole thing over. I wanted to stop by this morning to see if you would like to go to dinner tonight. There is some special kitchen take-over happening at the Little Café and a friend of mine is the chef, so she offered me a couple of tickets."

Steph's mind was reeling over the partial argument they seemed to be having that suddenly turned into a real conversation about things between them. "Ah... I guess so."

"You guess?"

"I mean, I would love to." Steph smiled, letting go of her other feelings about what was just said between them and focusing on the invitation.

"Perfect. I'll see you there at 8." Dawn stood from the chair and glanced back only once before exiting the office.

Steph waited a minute or two once she was gone before heading to the lunchroom to find Julia. She wanted to make sure Dawn was out of the building in case another interaction made it weird for either of them prior to their date that evening.

She popped her head into the breakroom. "I'm ready whenever you are," She said to Julia before tapping her hand on the doorframe and making her way back down the hall to her office.

***

Steph was barely situated in her chair when Julia entered carrying two cups of coffee and placed one gently in front of her. "You made me coffee?"

"One cream, one sugar, right?" Julia smiled.

"Yeah, thanks. I could really use this."

"Dawn is visiting you at work now? Things must be getting serious," Julia teased.

"That's not quite...I mean, no it's not getting serious, I don't think. I haven't seen her in over a week."

"Funny, I thought you were super into her and you would be cleaning out a drawer for her by this time, at the very least."

"I told you, I have no interest in rushing into anything with anyone right now." Steph clapped back.

Julia raised her hands in front of herself in surrender.

"Sorry, I didn't know it was such a touchy subject. So, you have been avoiding her and she showed up here to make sure you couldn't?"

"Something like that. Something happened and I freaked out and I just wanted to slow things down, so I was just putting off seeing her for a while. And, yes, she decided to show up here to corner me about what was going on and now we have a date tonight."

Julia's teasing tone changed as she frowned. "So that is still a thing then?"

"It seems so. I do like her but," Steph smiled back trying not to think about what Dawn had said about her feelings for Julia and finding herself a little flustered in the effort. "There are just other things that are making it more complicated." Steph shook her head, chasing away the thoughts. "So, what did you want to meet about?"

"You wanted to meet with me, remember? About how we are going to handle the coverage of the court case for the Closet Murders?"

"Right, yes, of course I did. So, I think the main thing I wanted to discuss is whether you think Kerri is up to staying on the story now that we know that Doug Peters is the killer and with her relationship with his wife," Steph said, matter of factly.

"I don't think there is anything in this world that would make Kerri want to get away from this story. In fact, I think she is even more invested now that Doug has been arrested. And she may have a relationship with Summer, but, if I understand correctly, she only met him one time so she has no prior relationship with him."

"Okay, that's great. I didn't want to have to pull her from it, but I also don't need my photographers or reporters having outbursts in courtrooms because they are too close to the case."

Julia chuckled a little. "I don't think you need to worry about that. Kerri is so calm for the most part that the idea of her having a public outburst for any reason seems unreal to me, first of all. Secondly, following this through to the end will probably give her some closure. Was that all?"

"One more thing." Steph opened the top drawer of her desk and pulled out an envelope. "Here is the court schedule. The trial gets underway tomorrow and they have it scheduled for the next two months."

"Perfect. I'll get a copy of this to Kerri this afternoon, but I'm willing to bet she already knows." Julia sat reading over the schedule.

"Well, get back to work then." Steph shooed at her.

"You got it, boss." Julia jumped up from her chair and paused at the door before opening it. "We can talk more about Dawn later if you like."

"Thanks, but it's okay. I'll figure it out."

***

Steph strolled across the street to the Little Café where Dawn was waiting outside for her. She ran her hands through her hair, casually tucking it behind her ears before adjusting her dress shirt under her jacket and nodding at Dawn that she was ready to go in.

The café was barely recognizable as the place where she got her morning coffee with tables moved around, several additional ones added and fancy tablecloths and table settings sprucing the atmosphere to that of a high end restaurant.

Steph looked down at the obvious red sneakers on her feet and smirked. "I'm suddenly feeling a little underdressed for this occasion."

Dawn rubbed her hand across Steph's shoulder blades and gripped the back of her neck. "You look great."

The waitress ushered them to a table near the window and Dawn was already waving at someone and walking away before Steph had even sat down. Steph watched as she animatedly talked with a woman a couple of tables over and then gestured in her direction a couple of times before both women made their way over.

"Steph, this is one of my best friends, Kate Brown. We have known each other since middle school, and she is the one who gave me the tickets for tonight."

Steph sized her up as about five foot seven with long dark hair and a bit of mysteriousness about her. "Hi Kate, nice to meet you." Steph stood and extended her hand.

"Nice to meet you too, finally. Dawn has been telling me all about you, but I was starting to think you were fictional."

"Oh, really, she has been talking about me?"

Dawn shot Kate a look, "Well…"

"All good things, I swear. It's been a while since any of us have seen her take dating seriously so we may also be pressing for details too." Kate poked Dawn in the ribs, teasing. "I hear you are a reporter?"

"Sort of. I'm the editor and chief over at the Observer?"

"Oh, she didn't tell us you were the boss. That's impressive."

"I guess. It means some crazy hours at times, but I enjoy it." Steph shrugged.

"Ah, yes, I know all about crazy hours as a chef. Speaking of which, I should get back in the kitchen, this is my event after all."

"Well, it was nice to meet you, Kate." Steph sat back down and began placing her napkin across her lap.

"I'll be right back." Dawn smiled and wandered toward the kitchen with Kate.

Steph watched them as they spoke, noticing a flirty vibe between them in the way Kate touched Dawn's arm as she laughed and casually placed her hand on her hip to whisper something in her ear. She could feel her blood pressure rise at the interaction but convinced herself that she wasn't allowed to be jealous about it at this point in their relationship. After all, she was the one that was putting distance between them since they had sex. Besides, she had no idea what their history was, just that Dawn had called her one of her best friends and it wasn't weird for best friends to be touchy feely, right?

Steph pushed the feeling down as Dawn returned to the table. She wanted nothing more than to ask if Kate was more than an old friend, but as unlike her as it was, she refrained, hoping instead that Dawn would bring it up and give her more details on their past. Steph knew that she had no right to make accusations after the way she had dismissed Dawn that morning when she mentioned that she saw something between her and Julia.

They sat mostly in silence through the appetizer and until the main course was served. Steph pushed the food around her plate, taking a deep breath a couple of times as if to speak, but just lowered her eyes and stared back at her plate. Finally, Dawn dropped her fork dramatically, forcing Steph to make eye contact.

"What is wrong with you tonight? I know this was a little last minute and all, but you have barely said two words to me since we got here."

"Sorry, I guess my mind is somewhere else," Steph

replied meekly, glancing toward the kitchen.

Dawn followed her eyes and huffed, "Is this because I introduced you Kate?"

"No, not that, well, that is some of it," Steph checked around the room to make sure she didn't know any of the other customers, or that if she did, they hadn't overhead. "It's more about how you were with her. I know we have only been out a few times and I have no right to be jealous and I don't think that is what this is, but it certainly seems like there is more between you than friends."

"You got all that from the 30 seconds we were talking? That's interesting."

"I lived with a cop for five years, I was bound to pick up a few things about reading body language," Steph retorted.

"I don't think it will make you feel any better to know, but it was something, once. When we were just kids, really, and it was just a nightmare. It was one of those moments where we figured out pretty quickly that we should be friends and nothing more. I'm really just glad that we figured it out and I wound up with the best friend that I have today and that we didn't let it go on until we hated each other or something." Dawn reached across the table and laid her hand on top of Steph's. "I can promise you we will never again be anything more than friends and I know that we are a little flirty with each other but there is no sexual chemistry between us at all. Just platonic love." Dawn shrugged her shoulders.

Steph just nodded and lowered her head, once again pushing around the food on her plate. She suddenly looked up as if she had a brilliant idea, put down her fork, wiped her mouth with the napkin in her lap and stood from the table. "I don't think we should see each other anymore. I'm not ready to be dating and I'm doing this for the wrong reasons." As the words fell from her mouth, Steph felt like she could breathe for the first time in weeks. "I'm sorry. It's just bad timing."

Dawn just stared up at her, her jaw slightly open and a look on her face that Steph wasn't sure if it meant she was going to cry or if she was just overly confused. Steph waited only a minute to see if she would say anything before turning and walking out of the restaurant, almost skipping in fact, with a weight off her shoulders she didn't know was keeping her down.

CHAPTER 16

After a couple of weeks alone, Steph had found a new confidence and clarity she hadn't realized she was looking for. That confidence was boosted again when she walked into the office exactly one month after she had submitted Julia and Kerri for the national journalism award to find a letter on her desk stating they had won.

With as much calm and composure as she could muster, she walked down the hall to Kerri's office where she found both her and Julia sitting behind her desk, looking through a number of photos from their trip to court the previous afternoon.

Steph put on as stern a voice as she could muster. "Good morning ladies, I need to see you both in my office as soon as possible." She folded her arms across her chest and waited for them to look up.

Kerri was the first to react. "No problem. Did we do something wrong?"

"This is a conversation for my office." Steph had all she could do not to smile and laugh as she quickly turned and headed down the hall to wait.

Within a minute the pair of women were standing before her, office door closed and wearing concerned looks that they were about to be called out by the boss. Steph could almost feel their nervous energy and just allowed them to stand in silence for a few minutes.

"Okay, get to the point. What did we do?" Julia finally blurted out.

Steph finally allowed a burst of laughter she had been holding back and could only laugh harder when she saw Julia and Kerri's reaction change from nervous to confused. She struggled to catch her breath, placing a finger in the air to ask for a minute and when she realized she was just going to keep laughing, she walked back to her desk, picked up the letter and handed it to Julia.

Julia read it quickly and passed it to Kerri whose eyes widened as they worked their way down the page, quickly absorbing the words upon it. She dropped the page on her lap and glanced between Steph and Julia, both grinning from ear to ear.

Steph leaned against the desk, crossed one foot over the other and folded her arms across her chest smirking. "Congratulations. I'm so proud of the both of you."

"We should go out and celebrate. How about Leroy's bar tonight after work?" Julia punched Kerri in the shoulder and grinned up at Steph.

"I think a celebration is in order. Just remember that although it is just the two of you being credited, there is a whole team out there that contributed to your success."

Julia stood from her chair and made her way across the office to stand right beside Steph. "Of course there is. We should ask around and see who wants to come out. You'll join us, right? You haven't been out of the house since you broke up with Dawn." She placed her hand over Steph's on the edge of the desk.

Steph quickly pulled away and moved to put the desk between herself and Julia. "We'll see. I have a lot of work to do and I really don't know what time I will get out of here."

Kerri stood and moved toward the door of the office. "Sounds great. You should definitely come, Steph, it won't be the same without you there. After all, we wouldn't be here if not for you."

"Thank you, Kerri, I will do my best to make an appearance."

"I should get back to work. I have some photos to compile for that piece on the new mayor." Kerri slipped out of the office and closed the door behind her, leaving Julia and Steph alone.

"So, how are you doing with the breakup? I know it has been a couple of weeks now. Are you seeing someone new, tried out the dating site again or anything?" Julia blurted.

"I'm just fine about the breakup, I broke up with her, remember?" Steph snapped back.

"Woah, sorry I asked. I was just trying to be a good friend. Why is it that every time I ask about your life you jump down my throat like I..."

"I'm sorry," Steph interrupted, quickly realizing Julia was right. "I don't know why I do that. I'll try and be better." Steph kicked her foot across the carpet of her office rug.

Julia huffed and crossed her arms over her chest. "Okay, so now that we have that clear, you didn't answer my other question. Are you seeing someone else and I will add, why did you break up with her anyway?"

"The timing was just wrong. I felt overwhelmed by being with her when I knew she was looking for something serious and, looking back, I was falling into a full-fledged relationship again without even realizing it I think. It was actually a relief to end it and just be on my own for the last little while." Steph shrugged.

Julia giggled and walked behind the desk, placing her hands on Steph's shoulders. "So, it didn't have anything to do with me then?"

Steph's body shuddered at the touch and she could feel her face flush as she drew in the heat from Julia's hands. She sighed, "How many more times do we have to go over this? You need to stop being such a tease with me. It makes it really hard for me to keep our friendship, but more than that, it is just really confusing when you flirt with me and ask me things like that and then I see you dating a half a dozen girls a week."

Julia released her hands from Steph's shoulders and sat on the edge of her desk, looking intently into her eyes. "We have been over this, but you don't seem to listen to me. Also, I just want you to know that I haven't been out with anyone in weeks. I got tired of wasting my time with women that I was only using to make myself feel better. I was just trying to move on from something and that wasn't the way to do it after all."

"So, you aren't even dating right now? That seems so out of character. I've known you for close to two years and I don't think I have ever seen you without a date on a Friday night."

"It's time for me to start being more selective. I'm 27 years old for God's sake. I can't do this forever and I'm ready to settle down a little, see how that feels." Julia shrugged.

"I was your age when I met Nicole and started to feel the same way I suppose. Not that I hadn't been in long term relationship before that, just that I hadn't considered them to be something I was going to be in for the rest of my life." Steph paused for a moment. "So, have you ever been in a relationship like that at all? A long term one, I mean."

"Oh, I didn't mean that. I have, just not in a long time. I was with my college girlfriend for three years, but I didn't want to leave here and she wanted to see the world. Not that it would have lasted anyway. Once we were out of school, we both became very different people. And I have been in a couple of relationships that lasted six months or more, but I decided a long time ago that I wasn't going to waste my life with someone that wasn't right for me; anyone that I had to argue with regularly or a person that didn't understand my life and career."

"I get that. I think that is what I liked about Dawn, that she understood the kind of life that I was living and what it meant on the demands of my time and how unpredictable it can be sometimes. I'm glad I realized early that it wasn't enough for her to feel that way and just because it was one of the biggest problems in my relationship with Nicole, it shouldn't be the main thing I was looking for in someone new."

"Exactly, it is important, but it should be a bonus, not a main trait that you choose someone for." Julia grinned. "I really like being about to talk to you like this. Just put it all on the table and know that we understand each other."

Steph sighed. "I know what you mean. I don't think I have ever had someone that I could just be totally open with about all the aspects of my life. Especially not someone who was going to actually understand my feelings about certain things, mostly work related and how I have to be able to shut off and just deal with those things when they happen."

"Right? I can't tell you how many exes have tried

to tell me that I had no empathy because I was excited about a story that meant someone was hurt or a building burned down or something. It's impossible to explain to people who don't do what we do that it is normal to put the people's feelings on the back burner and be excited about what is happening in the moment."

"Anyway, I shouldn't be keeping you. People are going to start to talk." Steph leaned back in her chair.

Julia shook her head. "No one is going to talk about anything happening between us because we had a long meeting. I thought you were moving past this?"

"That isn't what I meant. I was more thinking they would be wondering why we had to meet for so long and you looked so pale and worried when you walked through the door. I'm just thinking they will start gossiping that you are getting fired or something."

"Sure, I bet that is exactly what you meant," Julia replied sarcastically. "Okay, I'll go, but only on one condition."

"And what might that be?"

"You have to come out for a drink with us tonight to celebrate. And don't give me any 'I'm the boss and shouldn't do that' kind of stuff. I think it would mean a lot to everyone if you made an appearance. I know it would mean a lot to me." She paused. "And to Kerri, of course."

Steph sighed in exasperation. "I will do my best to make an appearance."

"That's what you said before. It sounds like a cop-out to me. What could possibly be so pressing that you can't take an hour to come celebrate with your co-workers?" Julia waited but Steph didn't reply. "Then I guess we will see you at Leroy's this evening." She turned and quickly left the office before Steph could say no.

CHAPTER 17

"Another crazy day in the news." Julia popped her head into Steph's office, "It's already after four and I don't think I've laid eyes on you all day."

"That's what happens when you are chasing a big story," Steph smiled. "Are we still on for Leroy's tonight?"

"Ah, yeah. I should remind Kerri about that. She didn't have any plans when I mentioned it earlier, but she did say she had to call her brother after work."

"Very well. I still have some things that I need to finish up before I can go, cross your fingers I get through it all or you won't be seeing me tonight after all."

Julia clicked her tongue in disapproval, "Now, now, just because you have the fancy office and title on your door doesn't mean you have to work harder than the rest of us, and it certainly doesn't mean you can't have a little fun."

"Yeah, yeah. I hear you, so get out of here a let me work!"

The idea of going to Leroy's with Julia made Steph smile and she found her mind wandering back to one of the first times they had gone out for drinks.

"See? I told you this would be fun!" Julia ribbed just minutes after they arrived at Leroy's Bar.

"So far, so good, I suppose. But I haven't even got a drink yet." Steph huffed and flopped back onto the couch in the corner of the room where she most often sat when she actually bothered to leave the house.

"Well, let me fix that for you." Julia grinned and headed toward the bar.

Steph just smiled back and checked her watch. She had a least two hours before Nicole was off duty so she wouldn't have to explain why she was home so late from work. She suddenly felt a twinge of guilt that she was out with Julia at all, but she was allowed to friends outside of their friends and Julia was a lot of fun to be around.

She shook her head to try to push away the feeling as Julia returned to the couch with two glasses of wine. She wasn't doing anything wrong and she needed to stop feeling like she was and just relax.

"Penny for your thoughts?" Julia quipped as she flopped onto the couch.

"Just work stuff, you know," Steph lied. She wasn't about to even mention Nicole's name to Julia.

"If you say so." Julia shrugged and swallowed down half of her drink in one go. "It's a shame you didn't want to go dancing."

"I told you, I'm a terrible dancer. Besides, isn't this a nicer way to hang out and actually be able to talk to each other?"

"I guess. It just reminds me of my school days, sitting in a sports bar trying to finish up some story for class that I would never waste my time on now." Julia chuckled. "Can you believe there was a time that I thought I wanted to be an entertainment reporter? I mean, who did I think I was and where did I think I was going to live that was going to make that a real thing?"

"Entertainment?" Steph smiled. "That is a good one. I can just see it now, Julia Demendo hanging out on the red carpet, chasing celebrities like the paparazzi in her backwards cap and three-day-old t-shirt with Cheetos dust smeared down the front."

"Hey! What makes you think I would be a pig in this scenario?" Julia nudged Steph in the shoulder, pushing her back into the arm of the couch.

"Well, after spending all that time hiding in the bushes to get a photo of the only famous person in this town, I would guess that you would have given up on hygiene," Steph laughed.

"Ha, ha. Well, I guess it is a good thing that I settled in as a crime reporter then. I dare you to find a single day when I show up with a hair out of place."

"Well now, I didn't mean to offend you." Steph started, but quickly stopped as Julia began to laugh.

They laughed until Steph's jaw hurt, downing at least three glasses of wine apiece before Steph looked down at her watch again. Just 20 minutes before Nicole would be home. She jumped from the couch and threw on her coat.

"What's the rush? You have somewhere else to be? Or are you just going to turn into a pumpkin if you aren't home by midnight?" Julia teased as Steph checked her pockets to ensure she had everything.

"I just realized how late it is. I should get home," Steph said, trying not to sound panicked as she checked her watch again.

"Sure thing. I mean, I won't keep you if you really want to go." Julia's expression changed from joking to serious. "We should really do this again sometime." She reached out and took Steph by the hand. "I had a lot of fun."

Steph just looked at where their fingers now met, and gently shook Julia's grasp away before turning for the door. "Yeah, we should. Definitely, we will do this again." Steph smiled shyly and once again swallowed back the feeling of guilt as she headed for home.

At ten to seven Steph finally locked her computer and grabbed her coat to head to the bar. Most of the lights were off in the office when she closed her door and walked toward the elevator. There were still a couple of offices lit in the editor's hall with those finishing up last minute story submissions and the overnight editor just getting started for the day, but the building was quiet, even compared to first thing in the morning.

Steph wandered down the couple of blocks to the bar, found a group of her reporters just arriving as well and joined the group as they entered the almost deserted bar. Steph could see the bartender's face drop when she saw them arriving. There was a nervousness building in her chest as her eyes met Julia's once again and she was greeted with another small mischievous smile. She followed the group to a set of couches near the back and stood at the end of one as they all got comfortable.

Steph leaned against the arm of the couch, as far away as she could get from Julia. However, Julia got up and forced Kerri and Steph to move down so she was beside Steph, pulling her down from the arm and onto the seat with her. Steph could feel the heat of Julia's body pressed against her and the knot in her stomach started to grow. She promised herself that she wouldn't feel this way anymore and that she wouldn't let Julia's teasing get to her, because that is all it was, teasing.

The conversation turned to television and Steph tried to focus on the chatter about what was new that fall and what people thought would be renewed for another year. Julia clapped at one suggestion, dropping a hand casually back into Steph's lap. Steph scanned the group, but no one seemed to have noticed what Julia was doing as she ran her fingers along the inside of Steph's leg.

Steph tried to remain calm, she wanted every one of these touches, but she didn't want the world to notice her expression change, or the flush in her face the further up her leg Julia let her fingers travel. She shuddered briefly and Julia squeezed a little in reassurance, keeping her focus solely on the conversation to try not to attract attention.

Steph's body longed for Julia's touch, almost willing her to be even bolder in that moment. She longed for the feeling of her flesh on her own bare skin, to finally know what it would be like to feel the press of her lips and her gentle caress. Julia gently stroked between her thighs and Steph could feel her wetness grow.

She closed her eyes, probably for too long, as she allowed herself to imagine where this could end up, where she wanted it to end up. Her mind drifted to thoughts of throwing Julia onto her bed and carefully pressing her lips against her body, being certain not to miss a single inch. Steph opened her eyes to shake away the images. She bit her lip to try to stay calm before quickly pushing Julia's hand away and jumping up from the couch.

The crowd turned to look at the flustered Steph. "Ahh, sorry guys but it looks like I'm going to have to cut this evening short. I just remembered that I have a couple of things to do at the office that I really shouldn't put off until tomorrow."

Julia stood beside her, folding her arms across her chest. "Anything I can help you with?"

Steph swallowed hard as Julia grinned at her once again. "I think this is something I have to do on my own. Besides, I don't want to pull you away from all the fun."

"You know, sometimes it's okay to ask people to do things for you. I really don't mind giving you a hand with whatever it is." Julia winked.

"Stay. Enjoy your evening." Steph turned and walked toward the exit, stopping to grab her jacket at the coat check before standing on the bridge of the bar, trying to catch her breath before heading home.

The door flew open behind her. "Is it something I did? I have tried to be subtle and it seemed like you didn't even notice so I just thought this was a great time to be a little less than. I'm sorry if I pushed too far. I wouldn't want to do anything that you didn't want." Julia folded her arms over her chest, shivering in the cold night air.

"No, no. I really do have to check on a couple of deadlines and organize some emails to get back on track with this story I'm working on." Steph took a few steps across the parking lot before turning to look back at Julia. "And trust me, if I didn't want it, it would have been stopped long before that." She blushed.

"Glad to hear it. I have to drop back to the office to pick up my gear for an early press conference before I head home so I'll check on you while I'm there. Make sure you aren't working too hard." Julia smiled.

"Sure thing. See you in a little while." Steph shook her head as she walked away. Now she actually had to go back to work that evening.

Steph sat behind her desk and opened Yahoo games. She needed to kill some time before Julia showed up to check on her and she really didn't have any work to do. It was close to an hour later when she heard singing from down the hall and quickly closed the game and started scribbling on her notepad to make it look like she was taking notes.

Julia poked her head around the corner of Steph's partially open door. "Truth time." She stepped into the office and stood across from Julia.

"What do you mean?" Steph said, suddenly defensive.

"Well, I have a strange feeling that you didn't have a real reason to be here tonight. Tell me, did you make up this excuse just to get away from me?"

"You want the truth? I can't handle all the teasing! I know you get a kick out of making me squirm but tonight was a little over the line, considering you have no real interest in me."

Julia laughed. "Is that what you think? I may have been just teasing you early on, but only because you said you didn't want to get involved with someone at work. I had feelings for you from the start, but I knew that acting on them was only going to get me hurt. I couldn't help but be a little playful with you and see if I could change your mind."

"But what about all those girls you met online? Or the night that you made a play for Kerri? How could you do that if you were interested in me?" Steph tapped her pen against the desk, watching it bounce as she spoke.

"You said you weren't interested. What was I supposed to do, hang around like a lovesick puppy and hope you changed your mind? I'm not that kind of person."

The pen flew out of Steph's hand, landing beside the desk. She rolled her chair over to pick it up, but Julia was already on her knee to retrieve it. Face to face, they just looked at one another for a moment before Julia licked her lips and Steph felt compelled to do the same as Julia reached up and grabbed her by the front of the shirt, pulling her closer.

Steph leaned forward, pushing the chair out from under her and grabbed Julia around the waist, guiding her onto the floor of the office. Julia kept her grip on Steph's shirt, and pulled her down on top of her into a kiss. Steph gasped, pulling back a little, but Julia ran her hand along the back of Steph's neck, holding her close enough to kiss her again.

Steph's arms began to tremble as she was holding herself in a partial push up, keeping just a slight separation between their bodies and she knew she would have to give in. She gently allowed her body to press onto Julia's and kissed her more deeply. With one swift movement, Julia rolled her over, pinning Steph to the floor before kissing her again.

There was a loud bang in the hallway and Steph pushed Julia away, realizing that her office door was still open. Just pulled herself up from the carpet and brushed herself off, trying to act casual as Julia did the same. Her hair was now a messy ponytail and she knew she didn't have time to fix it before acknowledging whoever had come into the office.

Kerri was shaking her head and chuckling to herself as she walked through the door. "Well, well. It's about god damn time, you two. I didn't know how much longer any of us could deal with that tension and I've only known you a couple of weeks."

Steph looked nervously at Julia, "What are you talking about?"

"I didn't take either of you for sex at the office kind of people, but hey, to each their own, and you are the boss." Kerri grinned.

"You have this all wrong. That isn't what was going on here. Why would you think that?" Steph could feel panic tightening in her chest.

"Well, the first tip off was the way you both reacted

to my presence, followed by the lipstick you both have smeared across your faces, your hair is usually pristine, but it is coming apart like it was pressed to a pillow, or the floor. I'm not one to judge, and believe me, this has been a long time coming."

Even Julia was starting to blush. "We are not sex at the office kind of people. We just kissed a little." She hung her head, glancing back at Steph for approval to continue. "Kerri, please don't say anything to anyone about this? We haven't really even figured it out."

"Oh shit, I walked in on your *first* kiss? Oh god guys, I'm so sorry," Kerri stammered, "I'll get out of here, let you get back to figuring it out. I would recommend that you close the door, though," she winked, "wouldn't want just anyone walking in."

"So, is this the part where we have to process everything that just happened? Or, instead, can we maybe go back to where we were before we got so rudely interrupted? This time with the door closed?" Julia placed her hand on Steph's cheek, gently rubbing her thumb along her lower lip.

Steph pulled away, turning her back to Julia. "I still don't know if I can do this. Everything I said about this being too much is true. I shouldn't date someone I work with, I sure as hell shouldn't date someone that is under me at work and I don't know how people would react to me dating anyone at work, never mind a woman. How would I even begin to make people okay with it?"

"Why are you so worried about what other people will think? We can't even be sure there is more than just attraction behind this right now. We like each other. Why can't we just see what happens and deal with the fallout from there?"

"Can you just promise me one thing?" Steph turned around to face Julia again, placing her hands on Julia's hips.

"I can try." Julia slid her hands over Steph's shoulders and around her neck.

"This needs to stay between us for now. Until we figure things out, I mean. I don't want the wrong people to hear about it before I am ready."

"I can respect that, within reason. I won't go back in the closet for anyone. What do we do about Kerri? She already knows." Julia ran her fingers along the middle of Steph's neck.

"I have a feeling she isn't going to blab about it. I know you guys are getting close, and I know she is going to have questions, but please, no details to anyone until we know where this is going."

"On one condition."

"You just love to give me conditions. What is it this time?"

"You have to agree to a date with me." Julia leaned back into Steph's hands, looking for the answer in her eyes.

"I can do that. How about I make you dinner. Tomorrow night? It's my day off."

"It's a deal." Julia pulled Steph's face closer and gently kissed her again. "I guess I'll see you then." She grinned sheepishly before exiting the office.

CHAPTER 18

Steph got up early and headed out to the store to pick up things she would need to make her mom's special chicken parmesan for dinner with Julia that evening. She wasn't in the habit of keeping much in the house in the way of groceries with the hours that she worked, so she would need almost everything, including the spices.

Steph had only ever made the dish once as she ordered out six nights a week and if it wasn't take-out it was probably a frozen pizza because she was too lazy to leave the house. She stood staring at her list and the spices on the shelf in the aisle when Summer approached, startling her from her thoughts. "Hey! Glad to see you are out and about. Kerri said you were doing better, but I didn't realize you were getting out of the house."

"Steph, right?" Summer replied, trying to place the face of one of Kerri's co-workers.

"Right, Kerri's boss. I'm sorry, I know we only met once I shouldn't have assumed that you would remember." Steph extended her hand for Summer to shake.

"This is actually the first time Kerri has let me out without following me." Summer laughed. "Not in a weird way or anything, but she has been a little over-protective until now. I guess she figured she should loosen the apron strings a little with me going back to work next week."

"Wow, I would say that is fast, but I know what it takes to keep me away from work and I would be out of my mind if I had been home on bed rest for as long as you have."

"Tell me about it. For the first couple of weeks, I couldn't even pick up my little girl, but Kerri has been a God send through all of this, and I guess I owe you a thank you for letting her move her hours around at work to help me out for so long." Summer smiled.

"Oh, my pleasure. I would want to be there for my person if something like that happened and I know that Kerri would have done anything to make it happen." Steph blushed as she watched Summer do the same.

Summer quickly changed the subject, "You seem a little confused, are you trying out a new dish?"

"Any dish is new for me. I don't really cook so I'm not sure why I thought cooking tonight was a good idea."

"There was a time that I thought I wanted to be a chef, personally. Is there something I can do to help?"

Steph looked between her list and the shelf again before handing the piece of paper to Summer. "Well, apparently I need all of these things and it seems like there are three kinds of every spice. How am I supposed to know which one to get? Like here, it says I need garlic, but do I want crushed? Powder? Salt? Maybe I should just quit while I'm ahead and order in for us."

"Ah, I see. You have a date that you are trying to impress," Summer chuckled. "Any reason you decided on this meal?"

"This is going to sound silly, but my mom used to tell the story of the first time she made it and it was the first time that she cooked for my dad."

"Wow, you really like this girl, hey?"

Steph didn't even stop to recognize that Summer had known it was a woman. "Yeah, I really do, and I really want to get this right. I suppose this has been a long time coming and I want to show her that I'm serious about it. I just put her through so much to get here. Not that she hasn't done the same to me in a lot of ways and, to be honest, I was pushing her away for all the wrong reasons really and I think I'm kinda trying to make up for that at the same time."

"I get it. I pushed Kerri away so many years ago when I never should have, and it took us way too long to find each other again. I made a bunch of mistakes when we finally did reconnect too, but I try to show her every day that I'm serious about making things between us work. I think she might even be ready to really move in with me."

"I thought you were already living together?" Steph said without thinking. "I'm sorry, I don't mean to pry, we barely know each other and here I am spilling my guts to you in the middle of the market and asking you all these personal questions."

Summer tucked her hair behind her ears and smiled, "It's okay. I don't mind. It's nice to have someone to talk to that understands a little about what I'm going through and knows Kerri enough to be able to talk to you about her. She has been staying with me to help out, but not in the same room. She wants to take things slow while I recover, and we have just fallen into a strange routine where it's almost like we are roommates. I don't really know how to make it get back to what it was starting to become before all of this happened."

"Have you tried just being honest with her? I know

that sounds silly, but sometimes the one thing you aren't doing that you think you are is just saying exactly what you want out loud," Steph offered.

"Sort of, I guess. I have tried to show her that I want more, but you are right, I haven't actually just said it." Summer paused, grabbed the garlic powder from the shelf and dropped it in Steph's shopping cart. "I would get fresh for the rest. But I always prefer the powder over having to crush the cloves. Just be careful how much you add."

"Thanks. You are a life saver." Steph smiled and took the list back from Summer.

"Thank you for the advice. I'm glad I ran into you."

"Anytime, and that isn't just lip service."

Summer reached into her purse and pulled out a card, handing it to Steph. "We should hang out sometime. My number is on there, or I suppose you could just talk to Kerri about it at work."

"Yeah, that would be cool. Well, I suppose I should get back to the list."

"Good luck with it, and I hope your date goes well tonight." Summer waved as she walked toward the check out.

***

It was a little over an hour later when Steph walked through the door of her house, juggling the grocery bags as she struggled to kick off her sneakers so she could get to work. She dropped the bags on the kitchen island and pulled an old recipe card from a drawer to check the first steps in the process.

Steph rooted through the cupboards for the right pots and pans and laid out the items she had purchased, just staring at the arrangement and the recipe for a while before throwing on an apron and attempting to get started.

It was a moment when she wished she could call her mother and ask for guidance on the process, but she knew there would be a ton of questions about why she wanted to make it in the first place and also shaming for the fact that she was over 30 and still couldn't cook for herself. The barrage of 'you will never make anyone a good wife' and the onslaught of 'are you seeing anyone' and 'you need to find a nice boy and settle down' was sure to follow.

Steph meticulously followed the instructions on the recipe card and was actually impressed with how it turned out as she placed in in the oven for the final baking. A quick glance at the clock told her she had just 30 minutes to shower, dress and clean up the kitchen before Julia arrived.

Steph decided to shovel all of the dirty dishes into the dishwasher to leave less to get done and headed for the shower. She threw on her radio, set to her favourite oldies station to try to distract her and calm her nerves as she rushed through the process and quickly towel dried her hair before wrapping the towel around her body and sitting on the edge of her bed to take a couple of deep breaths in the hope of bringing her heartrate down.

Another look at the time told her she needed to get a move on in case Julia was even a few minutes early. She threw on her darkest pair of jeans and her favourite button-down shirt, then checked her hair one final time in the mirror as the doorbell rang, announcing Julia's arrival.

Steph's hands were shaking as she turned the doorknob and stepped back to let Julia enter the porch. "Come on in. Dinner is almost ready. I'll get you a drink, white or red?"

Julia giggled a little. "White is good. Anything I can

do to help? It certainly smells good in here. I didn't realize you were a good cook."

"Truth is I'm not really. I barely ever have time to do it. I just wanted to impress you. Is it working?" She smiled coyly.

"I'll let you know when we see how it tastes," Julia replied as she followed Steph into the kitchen.

Steph carefully plated the food and placed it in front of Julia at the table. "So, we obviously don't have to go through all that uncomfortable small talk that would normally make for first date conversation."

"At least there is that. There is nothing worse than going through the whole get to know you part." Julia carefully cut a piece from her chicken and analyzed it before putting it in her mouth.

Steph watched in anticipation as Julia chewed. "Well? Impressed or not?"

Julia smiled. "Impressed, but I am always impressed by you. So, does this mean if we work out, I won't have to get all my meals from La Bistro anymore?"

"I wouldn't go that far. That is, unless you like this enough to eat it every day. It's pretty much the only thing I learned to make and most of that learning happened today. I'm just surprised nothing burned or came out under cooked. You don't cook either?"

"Not that I can't; I have many skills." Julia winked.

"Xena now, are you?" Steph shook her head at the reference. "Well, maybe that means you should be the one cooking for me the next time."

"Maybe I should. And I'm surprised you got the reference. No one ever does."

"Trust me, you can't stump me on anything gay or gay adjacent in pop culture. I spent most of my 20's watching and re-watching Xena and movies like But I'm a Cheer-leader and The Incredibly True Adventure of Two Girls in Love." Steph grinned as she remembered the many hours she had spent in front of her television to try to get a glimpse of someone like her.

"You know the thing I loved the most about Xena is that unlike a lot of fantasy type shows and even sitcoms of the time you didn't have to worry they were going to jump the shark. They had done that on day one so when it started to get really strange and off the wall you barely noticed. Watching it again now you can really see where it got incredibly weird though." Julia shook her head.

"Anytime it got really odd they just attributed it to the Gods anyway. Besides, it was as close to getting two women in love on television as we were going to get in that time period."

"Interestingly enough, I didn't even realize the sub-text at first. It wasn't until I re-watched it when I was a bit older that I could see what all the fuss was about. I guess I was only 15 when I first saw it, but I already figured out that I like girls at that point so you think I would have noticed." Julia shrugged.

"You already had it figured out at 15? Wow, I was really behind the times, I guess. I didn't even kiss a girl until I was seventeen, and even then, I thought I was just experimenting. I guess I didn't want to believe that it could be real, even though it was the only time I felt any kind of connection to another person." Steph bowed her head.

The swagger and confidence that was usually in Julia's voice drained. "It doesn't matter how old you were when you figured it out, it matters that you decided to live your life in a real way and love who you want to love. That's a hard thing to do at any age, I know it was for me. It's a hard thing to do every single day but I want to be happy and this is the only way that I know to do that."

"But you act like it is no big deal and you don't care what anyone thinks about it. How do you live so confidently and so bravely if you struggle with it so much?"

"Because I have to. The more I come across as confident, the less people bother me. I guess I acted like I was for so long that I became that person. It didn't happen overnight or anything and there are still moments when I can't pull it together and I come across as insecure and nervous, but I do my best to push that down." Julia reached across the table and placed her hand over Steph's. "It's not that nothing bothers me, and that people don't get to me with their sly comments and looks sometimes, I just have learned to brush it off and be the me that I want to be, regardless of their actions."

Steph refilled their wine glasses and cleared the plates from the table. "I wish I had your confidence."

"You do, you just don't apply it to your personal life the way you do to your work. I see you with the staff and when you are doing an interview and you are one of the most confident people that I have ever met." Julia moved behind Steph at the kitchen sink and placed her hands on her shoulders. "Thanks for supper, by the way. This was really nice, and a lot nicer and more intimate than going out to a restaurant somewhere."

Steph could feel the beads of sweat forming on her forehead at Julia's comment about intimacy and the feeling of her hot breath on the back of her neck. "I just want to make sure that I was clear that there are no expectations tonight. I just wanted us to be alone somewhere that we could really talk and feel secure that we wouldn't be interrupted."

"I don't have any expectations either. I'm just glad we are finally being real with each other." Julia quickly pressed her lips to the middle of Steph's back, wrapping her arms around her body.

Steph shivered and almost dropped the plate she was washing as Julia's hands stroked along her stomach and interlinked at her belly button. She took a deep breath, feeling the warmth of Julia's fingers through her shirt and tried to calmly place the dish in the drying rack on the counter before turning her body to face her.

Without thinking Steph leaned in and gently kissed Julia, lingering for a moment on the fullness of her lips to ensure she was left with a taste of her wine on her own. Julia looked up at her and grinned as she waited to see if Steph would make another move. Steph just kept focusing on her eyes, trying to decipher what Julia was thinking while she struggled with her own thoughts about what she wanted to happen next.

Before she could talk herself out of it, Steph slid her hand through the back of Julia's hair and pulled her into a deep kiss, feeling her lips move against her own and that her hands were shaking a little as they moved from clasped behind her back to thumbs pressed into her hip bone. Julia groaned a little as their tongues met and Steph felt her heart rate increase as Julia's hands now stroked circles over a small bit of skin that had become exposed on her hip.

Suddenly, Steph pulled back from the embrace, struggling to catch her breath while all of her thoughts rushed from her mouth. "I don't think we should take this any further tonight. It's not that I don't want to or anything, I just know that I will spend the rest of the week wondering if you are going to stay interested if we jump in too soon with your track record and all."

The smile fell from Julia's face. "I know that you are just ranting, and you didn't think about what you were about to say, so I'm going to do my best to ignore it and just reassure you that no matter what does or doesn't happen right now is not going to change how I feel about you. I realize you have seen a fairly steady parade of people come and go in my life, but this is not like any of that."

"You say that, but how can I be sure?" Steph bowed her head, feeling a little pathetic about her response.

"Because I'm telling you it's true and because I wouldn't be here tonight with you if that was all I was looking for. Look, we spent months going back and forth on dealing with the fact that we have feelings for each other, how that could or would impact the fact that we work together and what being together would look like. I wouldn't have gone through any of that torment if I wasn't serious about trying to make a go of this."

"I know you're right, but you just make me feel so insecure. I haven't felt like that before, maybe because I didn't care enough about anyone else at this stage to let it get to me or maybe because I always felt like I had the upper hand in a relationship, but either way I can't shake the fear that this will wind up a one and done."

Julia stifled a laugh. "Processing already, we are really in for something with this, aren't we? Okay, so I can say all of the things you want to hear to alleviate your fears, but I have a feeling that is only going to make you feel more insecure in the long run because the reality is, I can't make any promises about what will happen in the future. We like each other. There is nothing more to it than that. Why can't we just deal with that feeling, the one we are both having right now and work the rest out later?"

"You're right. I should just be focusing on the now and not what will happen in the future." Steph closed her eyes and pulled Julia back into a kiss, much more forcefully than she had before.

Julia pulled away this time, grasping Steph by the hands. "Just to be clear, I still don't want to rush things. I want you, don't get me wrong, but I want to make sure we are there and like, ready to take that step forward."

"Okay. Thanks for talking this out with me." Steph brushed her fingers along Julia's cheek.

"We can always talk things through." Julia looked up at the clock in the doorway of the kitchen. "With all that said, however, I believe it is time for me to make my exit." Julia kissed Steph quickly and headed for the porch with Steph right behind her.

"I had a really nice time tonight." Steph smiled shyly.

"Me too. So, I would love to take you out for a second date soon. Do you have any plans on Wednesday?" Julia winked.

Steph stuttered, trying to grasp what her schedule looked like for the week and whether or not she could make it work. "I just might be able to fit you in."

"La Bistro, 6:30. I'll pick you up." Julia kissed her again softly and left.

CHAPTER 19

When Steph woke on Wednesday morning, she was already anticipating her evening date with Julia. She found herself distracted during her weekly interview with the mayor for updates on public works improvements that had been going on in the city for well over a month, and distracted was not something Steph was used to being.

She shook it off and blamed it on the repetitiveness of the conversation and not that she was struggling to push Julia from her thoughts. Steph had noticed her mind wandering to the memory of Julia kissing her in her office consistently since their dinner. She was brushing her fingers over her bottom lip at the thought of it when she heard someone clear their throat in the doorway of her office.

Kerri just grinned and shook her head at the shocked look on Steph's face as she realized her presence. "Off in your own little world this morning, I see. I wonder what you could possibly be thinking about," She teased.

Steph let out an embarrassed laugh, "I'm sorry, were you standing there long?"

"Just a minute or so." Kerri closed the door and leaned against it, folding her arms over her chest. "I just came by to tell you that I will no longer need the apartment I've been renting through the company."

"That's great! I guess that means you are officially moving in with Summer? I'm so happy for you both. I know she really wanted this."

"I am. And I feel like everyone knew this was happening before I did."

"I may have run into her at the store the other day. She was very helpful in making sure I didn't screw up my dinner and she might have mentioned something about it while we were chatting. I hope that's okay."

"Totally cool. To be honest, I'm glad you two hit it off, or at least it sounded like you did from her end. She could really use a good friend. I think Doug may have pushed her to stop contacting any of the friends that she did have around here and I'm going to be a lot for some of her old friends to accept, so it would be nice for her to have someone that she can talk to."

"Yeah, it would be nice for me too. It seems I may have disconnected for too long from a lot of my old friends and then with my recent break up, I believe most of my more recent friends have taken her side."

"That sucks, but I understand. I think we have all been there. You can always talk to me if you need to, you know. I like to think I'm a pretty good listener." Kerri smiled softly to try to show her sincerity.

"I appreciate that, it just feels a little weird where I am your boss." Steph swallowed hard, making a quick decision. "While I have you, can we talk about what you saw the other night?"

"Of course we can. I would just like to start by saying that I'm happy for you guys. I have been watching you two look like the sexual tension was going to bubble over and explode for months. I know it seems cliché to say, but it was palpable to anyone with half a brain." Kerri chuckled.

Steph blushed. "I didn't realize it was so obvious. I guess I will have to work harder to make sure it isn't."

"I wouldn't. It's really sweet. Watching it unfold has been a welcome distraction for me over the past few weeks with everything else going on."

"Well, what I really wanted to say is that I would appreciate it if you didn't say anything to anyone about Julia and I. It's still really fresh and I don't know what is happening and I hadn't planned for anyone to know about it yet."

"No worries about that. I didn't even say anything to Summer, to be honest. It's really none of my business what is or isn't happening but if you want to talk about it, know that you can always come to me and I think Julia knows that too. She really is a great person. We haven't known each other that long, but it feels like I have known her my whole life and she has been really great to me with Summer being on bed rest for so long and everything."

"Yeah, despite the way she carries herself sometimes and the way she can come off to people, Julia is actually one of the nicest people I have ever met. You know, I once saw her spend three hours trying to coax a kitten out from underneath a bridge for a little girl who had accidentally let her out of the house?"

"That's amazing. Did she do it?" Kerri laughed.

"Yes, but not before crawling under there through the mud and pulling it out. I'm pretty sure she ruined one of her favourite shirts that day." Steph bit her lower lip thinking about how cute she had thought Julia was when she saw her covered in mud, including a smudge down her cheek.

"That's a great story. Well, I suppose I should get back

to work." Kerri stood, pushing the chair back from the desk.

"Great. And thanks for the ear. You can tell Summer that I will probably give her a call next week to get coffee or something."

Kerri had no more than closed the office door when Steph found herself drifting back into her daydream about Julia. The day seemed to drag on forever as she forced herself back to reality so she wouldn't find herself drowning in paperwork later that week. She had been pushing down her excitement for that evening's date since she opened her eyes that morning, two hours before her alarm clock.

Steph placed her coffee mug to her lips, discovering that it was empty for the second time that morning and huffed as she pulled herself from her office chair to make her way down the hall to get a refill. Every day she thought about getting a percolator for her office and every time she stopped to look at one in a store she realized that she would miss the break room run-ins with co-workers if she bought it, especially Julia.

The break room was empty when she walked in and flicked the switch on the wall to illuminate it. It was eerily quiet in the halls for a time of day that usually had reporters crashing into each other to get from place to place in a hurry to get the next big scoop. Steph shrugged her shoulders and filled her cup as close to the top as she dared without spilling it on the counter. She lingered in the room for a while, hoping someone would come in and strike up a conversation, but when ten minutes had passed and she still hadn't even seen anyone walking the corridor, she decided to investigate.

Steph made her way to the bullpen where she found

a large group huddled around the single television in the office, watching as police gave a press conference with the update on The Closet Murders. She quickly glanced around to see if Julia or Kerri were still at the office but was pleased to hear Julia's voice coming from the television, asking questions about the case.

She couldn't help but swell with pride when she heard the types of questions Julia was asking. Steph wasn't sure if she was proud of her little cub reporter, or if it was on a more personal level, but she was glad to be feeling positive about it all.

Her thoughts jumped to their plans for that evening and her face flushed as she tried to hold back a smile. She sauntered back to her office and closed the door to hide as much as possible until the day was over, and she could once again share that smile with Julia alone.

***

Steph kept her head down and tried desperately to focus on her work. She finally found herself wrapped up in a letter to the editor about the Closet Murders submitted anonymously to her email that had landed in the junk folder. It was surprisingly well written and seemed to include a few details she wasn't sure that she was aware of previously. Steph started to wonder if it could have been written by the killer, but shook the thought from her mind, "This isn't the movies," she muttered aloud to no one.

Steph closed the file and checked the clock to find it was already 5:15 and she needed to get home and get ready for her date. She stacked the papers on her desk neatly and locked her computer before standing and composing herself to have to chat with anyone who might be in the hall on her way out.

She marched toward the door like a woman on a mission and was grateful that no one tried to stop her to talk as she made her way out and into the parking garage. She jumped in her car and was about to drive away when a car came around the corner, screeching its tires on the turn and forcing her to slam on the brakes so she didn't side swipe it.

Steph gripped the steering wheel hard, her knuckles turning white as she did. She took a couple of deep breaths. She could hear her heart thundering. She couldn't think of anything that caused her heart to feel like it was beating out of her chest the way a close call in a car did. It was just a reminder to her that life was short and she shouldn't hold back in any part of it. In a few minutes she had calmed down a little and pulled out of her parking space to head home and wait for Julia, the thought of which made her heart race again, but in a different way this time.

She rushed in the front door and breezed past the answering machine with its light flashing for her attention to make her way to her room to throw on a fresh outfit for the evening. She wanted to try to keep it as casual as possible, show Julia what she was really like outside of work, and not look like she was trying too hard. She also didn't want to make too big of a mess of her room, so she meticulously refolded each rejected t-shirt and placed it back in the drawer. She was holding on to the feeling from the parking garage and hoped it would carry over into the evening.

Just as she pulled on a long sleeve plaid over her Guns and Roses t-shirt the doorbell rang, and Steph once again felt her heart skip a beat. It had been a long time since she felt this way about seeing someone and she allowed herself a little squeal of delight before running to the porch to open the door.

"Hey there." Steph blushed as she made eye contact with Julia.

Julia fiddled with her keys in her hand and grinned back. "Hey. You all set?"

"Just about. Jacket weather?" Steph quipped as she opened the closet door beside her.

"Sort of, but it probably will be later on." Julia raised her hands into the air, as though she could feel the weather.

"Perfect." Steph pulled her leather jacket from the closet, shut the door, shoved on her sneakers and threw it over her shoulder as she closed the door behind her and followed Julia to her car.

CHAPTER 20

Julia picked her usual table at the restaurant and sat with her back to the wall in the dark corner, forcing Steph to face away from the room. The pair sat in silence just grinning at each other for a few minutes until their server arrived with menus.

"Do we even need the menu? I think even I know your order by heart," Julia giggled uncharacteristically.

"You never know, I might surprise you!" Steph smiled back.

"I love a good surprise. Got any more of those up your sleeve for this evening?" Julia winked.

"Let's just wait and see how it goes, shall we?" Steph blushed and buried her face in the menu.

A few minutes passed as they silently read through the options that they had both pondered a hundred times before. Julia dropped the menu on her place setting, tucked her hands between her knees, leaned into the table and chewed softly on her bottom lip.

"Do you want to split an appetizer?"

"Well, that throws a wrench in everything I was just considering," Steph joked.

"Well, we don't have to. I mean, it was just a suggestion."

"No, no, what did you have in mind?"

"Well, the guacamole is calling my name, but it's a double dip platter and I know if I get it alone, I won't eat my main," Julia said with a vein of seriousness that Steph usually only heard her use in an interview.

"Well, you don't have to talk about it like it is the end of the world. The double dip sounds great to me." Steph smiled. "And just to shake things up completely, I think I will order tonight's special."

"But the special is striploin with mushrooms and mashed potato. How is that different than your usual?"

"It has mushrooms, for starters. And I usually get fries with mine."

"Okay, okay. You win, you are ordering something different." Julia shook her head and smiled.

They fell into easy conversation after that, avoiding conversations about work with the exception of a little gossip about Kerri and Summer and Steph's encounter with Summer at the grocery store. She had been too nervous to think to bring it up when Julia arrived for supper on Sunday evening.

"I think they'll get together. It's just a matter of time, I mean, they already live together and everything. They are practically married now for God's sake, raising that baby together for months," Julia mused.

"I suppose. All I know is that Kerri has been kind of avoiding the subject of anything more than a friendship and after some of the shit that Summer has put her through in the past, I can't say that I really blame her," Steph huffed.

"Anyway, enough of the will they, won't they talk about them. We should head out of here, it's getting late."

"Oh," Steph glanced at her watch. "I guess you are right. Would you like to walk me home?"

"That sounds nice. It's not a bad evening and it's just a couple of blocks."

"I honestly wondered why you wanted to pick me up in a car to begin with," Steph laughed.

"I don't know, it just felt more like an official date that way." Julia smiled and slipped her fingers between Steph's, holding her hand softly as they walked down the steps of the restaurant and onto the deserted sidewalk.

They walked in silence to Steph's front door, stealing glances at each other as they went and neither wanting to speak for fear it would break the spell of the way they were feeling, just holding hands.

When they arrived on the doorstep, Julia finally released her grip on Steph's hand and turned to face her. "I just have to say, I had a really great time with you tonight. There is just something so simple about spending time with you outside of work these days. It's just really nice to have all of the pretense out of the way."

Steph looked at her, a little confused but decided to let it slide. "I had a great time too. And I was thinking about it on the way over here, but I have the morning off tomorrow, so I was thinking that maybe, if you don't have an early day, you might be interested in coming in, have a drink, continue our chat. I guess I'm just not ready for tonight to end yet. And here I am, rambling like an idiot instead of letting you speak."

Julia couldn't contain her laughter, "It's not that it is funny. I just think it is so sweet when you act all unsure of yourself like this. This strong, confident woman that I am so used to seeing reduced to babbling over asking me to come in?"

"Well, are you going to just leave me hanging? If you have to go, I understand." Steph managed to choke out.

"Not at all." Julia placed her arms over Steph's shoulders and kissed her softly on the cheek before whispering in her ear, "I just like to watch you squirm." Julia pulled away and looked Steph in the eyes before continuing. "Court doesn't start until 1pm tomorrow, so I'd love to come in."

Steph unlocked the door and escorted Julia to the couch. "I'll just get us some wine, if that's okay with you?"

"Sounds perfect. Hey, you have messages," Julia shouted after her.

"That's fine. Most people call me on my cell when they get the machine. Only my mother bothers to leave a message and god only knows what she wants. I don't want to have to deal with that right now."

"Got it. She doesn't have a great relationship with her mother," Julia ribbed.

"It's not that, it's just more that she is always on my case about working too much and not being settled down and going out to eat too often and, really, just about anything else that she doesn't like about the way I live my life."

"So, she is like every mother on the planet practically?"

"Yeah, I guess so." Steph handed Julia her glass of wine. "Anyway, that's enough about my mother. Talking about her kinda puts a damper on the evening."

"Sure thing. But we will have to talk about our families at some point."

"I know, just not this point, okay?" Steph took a long swig of her wine and a deep breath for confidence before sitting as close as she could get to Julia on the couch. "I haven't been able to stop thinking about you since the other night."

"Well, that makes two of us…" Julia paused, thinking over her statement. "I mean, I haven't stopped thinking about you either." She placed her hand on Steph's knee.

Steph unwittingly shivered at the touch, a warmth flowed through her body and woke up her senses as though she had been physically asleep until that moment. She placed her hand over Julia's and began gently running her fingers along her forearm.

This time it was Julia's turn to make the first move. She pulled herself up in almost a cat-like fashion, moving her body toward Steph on the couch. She pushed her back into the armrest and pulled her body over her so they were face to face.

Steph giggled a little, anticipating the feeling of Julia's lips and placed her hand at the back of her neck, inviting Julia to continue. She wasn't used to someone else making the first move, but it felt nice to know that she was with someone who was willing to.

They stared at each other for a moment before Steph couldn't take the anticipation any longer and pulled Julia's face closer and into a forceful kiss. She could feel Julia's hands tremble as she placed one on her waist, touching the bare skin where her t-shirt met her jeans, and used the other to brace her weight on the back of the couch.

Steph's own hands and core were also shaking as she struggled to hold her weight off the couch and keep connected in the kiss. Finally, she had to give in and pull away, gasping for air. Steph kept her eyes closed, feeling the weight of Julia's body, now pressing down on hers. She could only breathe and didn't want to look for fear that Julia was not smiling at her the way she hoped after that kiss.

She didn't have to wait long to find out how Julia felt about it as she eagerly pressed her lips to Steph's collar bone, pressing her body down harder as she fumbled to free her hands. Steph let out an unwitting groan at the touch and ran her hands through Julia's hair as she continued to move her lips along her neck to the base of Steph's ear causing her to shudder as she whispered into it.

"Is this okay?" Julia allowed her lips to brush against her earlobe.

"Uh-huh." Steph bit her lip. "Damn, they are right! Consent is sexy."

Julia brushed her lips along Steph's cheek and placed her index finger under her chin, forcing them to be eye to eye. "I'm going to be asking for consent for more than this."

Steph looked her in the eyes and even if she couldn't see the rest of her face, she would have known that Julia was wearing her best mischievous smile. She kissed her quickly before speaking. "Not to be too bold, but should we move this to the bedroom?"

Julia pulled back slightly, searching Steph's face for reassurance. "Are you sure you are ready? No more concerns about what happens after?"

"Oh, I have concerns, but I want this, and I am ready, and I know that whatever happens it will be okay." Steph squeezed her hand and smiled. "And if this really is going to be our first time," Steph choked on the words and swallowed hard. "I don't want it to be a quickie on the couch. It should be more than that."

"Oh, I think it will be so much more than that." Julia grinned.

They walked hand in hand down the hall to Steph's room, neither of them speaking or making eye contact. As soon as the door closed, Steph pressed Julia into it gently and wrapped one hand around her waist to pull herself closer, running her other hand up the back of the door to support her weight.

Julia wasted no time, pushing her hands under the edge of Steph's t-shirt and running her hands up her back, unclipping her bra in one motion. She ran her fingernails along the flesh where the strap had been and down to her waist before grabbing the edges of the shirt and pulling it over Steph's head.

Steph paused for a moment, letting her bra fall to the floor beside the shirt and just looking into Julia's eyes before pulling her back into a kiss and fumbling with the buttons on Julia's dress shirt. She could feel the heat from Julia's hands as they gently caressed her back and shoulders. As she managed the last button and pushed the shirt away to expose her stomach, Julia forced them backward toward the bed, throwing Steph onto her back on the mattress.

She stood above her, smiling, as she finished removing her shirt, adding it to the pile of Steph's clothes on the floor and proceeded to undo Steph's jeans as she softly pressed her lips to her stomach. Steph groaned with pleasure, then covered her mouth to try to stay quiet.

Julia stopped and pulled back. "Are you trying not to make any noise?"

Steph looked up, her mouth agape but no words would come out, "Ah, uh, um," was all she could stutter.

"Please, don't. There is no one here that could hear you besides me, and trust me, I want to know that I am doing something right here and the best way I can tell is by your reaction. Don't hold it back."

Steph blushed, "I've always been the quiet type. I don't know if I know how not to be." She shied her eyes away from Julia.

"Just relax." Julia grasped her hand, kissing the tips of her fingers. "Just know that if you are enjoying yourself, it's okay to let me know."

Steph bit her lower lip and took a deep breath, trying to do as Julia said. "Okay, I'll try, but I'm making no promises."

Julia smiled and let go of her hand, running her fingers over Steph's stomach, she picked up where she left off, running her tongue along the edge of her jeans before starting again in the attempt to undo her belt.

Steph allowed herself to moan a little as she thought ahead to other places she wanted to feel Julia's tongue. She was almost shocked as she was pulled from the thoughts and back to reality as Julia ripped her jeans from her body and breathed a gentle kiss on the edge of the elastic of her underwear. It had been a while and with all the anticipation of this moment, Steph knew she was too excited already. She propped herself up on her elbows and motioned for Julia to meet her face to face.

Julia started to crawl up the bed toward her, when Steph put up the stop sign. "Lose the pants first," She managed to say, the blood filling her face with embarrassment as she asked.

"Yes ma'am!" Julia stood and saluted before dropping her jeans to the floor and crawling back onto the bed beside Steph. She brushed a strand of hair out of her face that had fallen from her usually perfectly quaffed ponytail and held her hand against her cheek. "Do you want to slow down?"

"Just a little," Steph admitted as she watched Julia's face fall a bit. "Not that I don't want to do this, cause I really, really do. I just want us to take our time." She placed her hand on the middle of Julia's chest. "Let me just blurt this out and have it said." She took a deep breath and focused her gaze on her hand. "I'm really attracted to you. Like, really, really attracted to you and if you keep doing what you are doing tonight is going to be over before it begins. I just want to make this moment last a little."

Julia giggled. "It's really okay. And, you do know that we can do this more than once, right?"

Steph composed herself, "Oh, I know." She rolled Julia over onto her back and placed her lips on the edge of her jaw.

Steph kissed down her neck and onto her exposed collar bone before making her way to the centre of her chest and running her tongue down between her breasts. She could taste the saltiness of Julia's skin and smell the sweetness of the perfume she had applied to that very spot. She licked her lips and looked up at Julia, who was watching her with anticipation.

Steph ran her thumb over Julia's nipple, and shivered at the softness of her skin before placing her mouth around it and gently flicking her tongue. Julia let out a slight moan and shifted her hips involuntarily. Steph knew she would soon have her at the same level of excitement and anticipation as she was already feeling. She placed a quick kiss at the centre of her chest before repeating the same action on the other side, this time also sliding her hand down Julia's stomach and pressing it softly between her legs. Steph could feel the heat of her arousal even through her underwear.

Julia reached her hands under the weight of Steph's

body and gently caressed her breasts. Steph fought the urge to tighten her jaw and moved to once again be face to face with Julia. She brushed her fingers under the edge of her underwear and grinned at the feeling of flesh that was soft as it was rarely touched.

Steph kissed Julia's chin. "Is this okay? Can I keep going?" She almost begged.

Julia smiled back at her, "Of course. And you are right. Consent is sexy."

Julia pushed Steph's body to beside her and began to mimic the actions Steph was taking. Steph felt as though she was staring so intently into her eyes that she might have been trying to get a glimpse into her soul. The intense eye contact drove back her insecurities and let her enjoy the moment more than she ever had in her life.

CHAPTER 21

Steph opened her eyes and stretched her arms and shoulders. She gently rolled over to ensure the previous night had not been a dream and that Julia was, in fact, still in the bed beside her. She was sure the smile she was still wearing had not even left her face while she slept. It had been one of the most amazing nights of her life and she never wanted the feeling to end.

Julia was still asleep, lying on her stomach with her bare shoulders exposed and her hair splayed out across her back as though it had been perfectly placed for a photo shoot. Steph picked up a strand and ran it through her fingers, wanting to touch her, but not wanting to wake her.

She glanced over Julia's shoulder at the alarm clock on the nightstand and knew that she couldn't let her sleep, as much as she wanted to. It was already 11am and she would need time to eat and get ready for work. Steph gently pressed her lips to her shoulder and caressed her arm, hoping to gently rouse her.

Julia moaned softly and turned her face toward Steph, eyes still closed but smiling just as much as Steph was. "Good morning," Steph said.

"Hey, you. Good morning, yourself." Julia almost

whispered as she finally opened her eyes. "How are you feeling this morning?"

Steph laughed. "So, so good. I'm really glad you spent the night."

"Well, it was like, 4am when you finally let me sleep and I don't know if there was enough left of me to walk home," Julia joked. "I'm glad you asked me to stay. It feels good to wake up beside you." She rolled toward Steph and placed her head on her bare chest.

"It feels nicer than I knew it could." She stroked Julia's hair out of her face and pressed her lips to the top of her head. "So, what is the protocol now? Should I offer to buy you breakfast?"

"What time is it anyway? I have to be in court this afternoon."

"Just after eleven. I didn't know how much time you needed to get ready."

"Oh, I've got plenty of time. Ten minutes to shower, dress and get out the door." She pulled herself even closer to Steph, pressing their bodies together and tangling their limbs together.

"Can I ask you something?" Steph posed, feeling the weight of the question but not really wanting to ruin the moment.

"You can ask me anything, always." Julia tipped her head up in anticipation.

"Was it okay for you? Last night, I mean. Was I good for you? You are just so much more experienced that me..." Steph averted her eyes, unsure that she wanted to see the initial response from Julia.

"You couldn't tell?" Julia placed her hand on Steph's face to force her to look her in the eyes. "Oh honey, experience isn't everything. You know that, right?" She paused, watching Steph's reaction. "Just because I've dated a lot doesn't mean that I've been with a ton of people who have a lot of experience or even know what they are doing at all. But trust me, you do. You know exactly what you are doing."

Steph bit her lower lip, processing what Julia was saying. "So, it was good?"

"If all my moaning and screaming last night didn't tell you that, I'm so sorry. But I don't fake it for anyone. In case I'm not making myself clear, it was more than good. It was incredible and I can't wait until it happens again."

Steph breathed a sigh of relief and let Julia once again melt into her arms. "Last night was amazing for me too, but I think this moment might even be better."

"At the risk of sounding too eager here, do you have plans this evening? I would love to see you again."

"I don't think so, although I never did check my messages, so I'll let you know later when I get up?"

"I wish we never had to get out of this bed." Julia placed her hand behind Steph's neck and softly stroked her fingers along the skin, causing goose bumps to form.

Julia's hand stopped and Steph could tell her breathing had changed, deeper now than before. She had drifted back to sleep in her arms and Steph could think of no better way to spend the next hour of her day than watching this beautiful woman sleep on her chest. She was about to doze off herself when suddenly she heard a noise in the house.

"Julia, wake up. I think someone is here. Did we lock the door last night, do you remember? I thought I did it when we came in, but maybe not." Steph sat upright in the bed. "I mean, the only person with a key besides me is…"

She could now hear the rustling of grocery bags in the kitchen and a woman's voice floating down the hallway, calling her name.

"Stephanie? Please don't tell me you are still in bed at this hour?" The voice was getting louder as it made its way down the hall toward the bedroom.

Steph shot Julia a look of sheer panic as the knob turned and she heard the click of the latch. She pulled the blankets up to cover as much of them as possible before the door swung open to reveal her mother.

"What in the name of the lord is going on here? This is an abomination! Get out of this house!" She moved toward the bed and practically pulled Julia from beneath the covers. "Get away from my daughter before you corrupt her any further." She yanked her by the wrist toward the door of the bedroom as Julia scrambled to grab her clothing from the floor. "You heathen! You have turned her to the devil and brought the greatest of sins down on this house!"

Steph could only mouth "I'm sorry," as Julia was dragged from the room. She jumped from the bed and threw on pyjama pants and an oversized sweatshirt before running down the hall shouting after them, "Mom, what are you doing? Mom, stop it, stop it right now."

Her mother released her grasp and turned and looked at her with a stare that she had not seen since she was a teenager and had done something her mother considered to be the end of the world, like come home after curfew or the time she had cut her hair in a sort of pixie cut. She would never admit it to anyone, but Steph was terrified of her mother, especially when she was mad, and had never once stood up to her.

Julia took the opportunity to try to dress herself, getting into her jeans as fast as possible and throwing her shirt over her back, even if she didn't have time to button it up. She was convinced she was about to be naked in the driveway for the whole neighbourhood to see, so at least this was an improvement.

Steph's eyes glanced between the glare of her mother and the panicked, confused face of the woman she had just spent the night with. "Mom, I want you to stop this right now. Julia didn't do anything wrong here and it is none of your business what I do in my own house."

"You listen here, Child! I brought you into this world and I will take you out. I should have known you were going down the path of darkness. You never go to church, there is nothing but silly posters and pop art on your walls. You don't even have a cross at the door anymore," Steph's mother poked her finger into her chest as she spoke, slowly driving her backwards into the living room and away from the door. She grabbed her by the shoulder and stared her in the eyes.

Steph was at a loss for words. Although she and her mother had never been the best of friends, she was a strong god-fearing woman who had never laid a hand on her until now. The events of the last few minutes were still spiraling in her mind and she struggled to grasp that it had actually happened.

"Nothing to say to me? Your father and I go out of our way to help you get this house and you go and bring evil into it." She shook Steph, bringing her back into focus.

"There is nothing evil about it," Steph whispered. She pushed her mother's hand away from her arm and drew her shoulders back to try to present a stronger front. She hadn't planned to defend her life today, but if this was how this was going to play out, then so be it. "You want to talk about God? That you think I'm the devil now and that because your religion says so that I am a disgrace in His eyes? Let me tell you something. I was told my whole life that God loved all of his children, no matter what. I was told that if you love your neighbour and follow the commandments then you are living a life that God would respect and that it was the pathway to heaven.

"Do you know why there is no cross at my door and no pictures of the virgin in my home? It's not because God doesn't approve of me. It's because your church doesn't, and do you know why that is, Mother?" Steph raised her voice to her mother for the first time in her life, "Do you know why I think that is?"

Now it was her mother's turn to just stare and await a response. She shook her head slowly and took a step back from Steph.

"Because they wanted to grow the church and people like me wouldn't make that possible. This, what you saw here today, this was not some person corrupting me. This is who I am, and I am so tired of hiding it and pretending to be something or someone else when I'm around you, or around anyone that isn't like me for that matter.

"I spent five years with the same woman. We built a life together, took vacations, made friends, built bonds, had a home and we were each other's family. That's over now, and a big part of it is because I spent that entire five years telling you she was my roommate, refusing to bring her to family events and if she did happen to come to something, she was simply introduced as my friend. No one knew her as the love of my life, my partner, my *lover*. She was just some girl that I shared a house with.

"She left me, partly because of my relationship with you, but mostly because I was terrified of this moment.

Terrified to tell you who I was and to live my life openly and honestly the way I should have. And do you know what most people would have done when they went through a breakup with someone that was practically a marriage? Most people would have called their mom. I didn't have that. All because you think God wouldn't like that I'm gay."

Her mother opened her mouth as though she was going to interrupt, but Steph held up her index finger and slammed her fist against the wall beside her.

"No, you don't get to stop me from saying any of this. After I thought my world was coming to an end and I had nowhere to turn for support I spent a long time trying to put the pieces back together. I realized that the things I was feeling for one of my friends was more than just a crush. I started to see the light again and know there was a way for me to find a different kind of happiness. This morning, you barged into my house, and not just my house, my bedroom, and you threw her out of here like some sort of piece of trash.

"Julia is not a heathen. I love her. And if you can't respect who I am and how I am going to live my life so that I can be happy, then you should just put on your coat and leave right now, because that makes you the heathen for not believing that God could love me anyway."

"How dare you? You need help. You're sick and you need help. You need someone who can make you normal again." Without warning Steph's mother pulled back her arm and slapped Steph across the face. "I...I...I'm sorry."

Steph held her face, feeling the burn where her mother's ring had impacted her cheek, and gritted her teeth. "Mom, I am normal. I think you are the one who needs help. I wasn't kidding. Get your things and get out of my house right now. I need to go see if Julia will ever speak to me again."

With that her mother made her way to the kitchen, picked up her purse and her jacket that she had placed on the table and made her way to the door. "You just wait. I'm going to go straight home and tell your father about this."

"You do that. But don't come back here until you are ready to apologize to me and accept me for who I am." Steph flopped on the couch as her mother slammed the door.

CHAPTER 22

Steph waited until she heard her mother's car pull out of the driveway and head down the street before she moved from her place on the couch. She checked the clock on the stove and realized she could still catch Julia before court if she hurried.

Steph threw on the first outfit she could find and rushed out the door so fast she almost forgot her keys. She jumped in the car and pulled out of the driveway like the house was on fire, then drove the three blocks to Julia's apartment. Main street was busy during the lunch hour rush and Steph was getting very impatient by the time she circled the block the third time in search of a parking space.

"Jesus, I should have walked, it would have taken less time," she muttered to herself as she turned the corner to make a fourth loop.

Finally, a space opened right in front of the restaurant and she pulled in, almost hitting another vehicle that had decided to try to back up the street to get it first. The other driver blew his horn at her and gave her the finger, but Steph didn't stop to have a fight with him. Instead, she ran straight to the door that led up the stairs to Julia's place and almost fell on her face twice as she sprinted to the top.

Steph started banging on the door while still trying to catch her breath. It was only 12:15, even if she expected traffic, Julia wouldn't have to leave for another 20 minutes to make it to the 1pm court docket. She banged on the door, calling her name. "Please be home. Please be home. Julia, if you are in there, please, I want to talk to you."

Steph stood alone in the hall for a few minutes, continuing to bang and call out with no response. She was about to leave when the door swung open and Julia appeared in nothing but a towel.

"Hey." Julia pulled the towel tighter around herself. "What do you want?" She said, not really in a dismissive way, but more defeated.

"I just want to talk. Can I come in?" Steph pleaded.

"I guess so. But you'll have to make it quick and talk while I get dressed. I have to go to work, remember boss?"

"I know, I know. I promise I will make this fast. I, ah…" Steph hesitated. An apology seemed empty for what she had just seen happen to this woman that she cared so deeply for.

"Well, just say you're sorry and get it over with," Julia shot out.

"That doesn't seem like enough. I want to say I'm sorry, but it feels like those are empty words. I mean more than that. I want to ask for your forgiveness, no I want to beg for it. I want to take the time to explain to you about my parents and tell you that something like this will never happen again. I want to look you in the eyes and have you believe me that every moment I spend with you makes me stronger and a better person and happier than I have ever felt in my life. You make me want to shout from the rooftops that we are together."

Julia focused her gaze on Steph, trying to read past her exterior. "Your words are the right ones, but I don't know if I can believe you." She stepped into the closet and threw her towel out onto the bed behind her.

Steph could see a slight outline of her naked frame through the gap in the door, causing her heart to start to race. "Words are not enough. They could never be enough. I can't even believe that this morning was real at this point. It just feels like a bad dream that I can't wake up from."

Julia reappeared, wearing grey pants, a grey vest and buttoning her white shirt underneath. "I haven't had to deal with that kind of shit from a parent since I was a teenager. I really thought I was past that part of life and past dealing with other people that weren't on the same page. I don't know if I can be in this with you if you aren't out with me."

"I know. Don't you think I know that? I had it out with my mother after you left. I told her everything. I told her that this is who I am and how I am going to live my life. I explained that you were more important to me than any God that says what we are doing is wrong." Steph stopped and sat on the edge of the bed, taking a deep breath, "I threw her out. I told her not to come back until she could accept that."

"Big words, Lady. I'm glad you stood up for yourself, but I just don't know if I can do this after today." Julia walked out of the bedroom and toward the front door. "She may have physically hurt me and said a lot of things that I thought I was done dealing with, but you are the one who hurt me the most when you didn't stop it from happening right away. You let her drag me out of the room, you let her almost put me out in the driveway, clothes in hand. I'm looking for an adult relationship, a grown ass person that I can share my life with. I can't go back to what things were like when I was in high school. Not for you, not for anyone."

"I know that. Really, I do. I want to make this right. Can you just let me try to make this right?" Steph was shaking and for the first time in a long time she was praying. She prayed that this wouldn't be the end of her and Julia.

"I'll have to think about it." Julia put on her coat and grabbed her keys from the coffee table in the living room. "Just give me some space, okay? I need some time to figure things out."

"Give you time. I can do time. How much time are we talking about here?"

"I don't know. I'll let you know, okay? Now please, I have to get to work." Julia ushered Steph through the door and followed her down the stairs to the street.

Steph stopped on the sidewalk next to her car and took Julia by the hand. "Just know that I really care about you and I don't want to end things like this."

"I care about you too, but it's not that simple. Time, okay?" Julia pulled her hand away and got into her vehicle.

"Yes, time."

***

Steph got back in her car and sat in the parking space for as long as her meter lasted. As soon as she saw the time flash with zeroes she pulled away and drove aimlessly for a while until she found herself in the parking garage for the Observer.

She wasn't sure why she had made her way to work, but something in the back of her mind told her to go to her office. When she walked in the door, the first thing she saw was Summer's business card sitting on her keyboard. The cleaners had been in earlier that day and they always put the things that fell under her desk on the computer so she would find it the second she came in.

Steph picked up the card and turned it over in her hands. Kerri was working and she knew that Summer was still off after the accident. She had said that they should get together for coffee sometime. Steph struggled with the idea of talking to someone else about what had happened, but if anyone would understand, it would certainly be someone who went so far in living a lie as to marry a man.

She dropped the business card back on the desk in front of the phone and picked up the receiver to dial. "I'd like to speak to Summer, please." She said when a voice answered.

The reply came quickly, "this is she, but the answer is no comment."

"No comment? I'm sorry? What?" Steph stuttered.

"You're calling from the Observer and I have already given an interview to one of your reporters and I don't have anything further to say. They sentenced him to life, and you want a statement, right?"

Steph shook her head and went back into apology mode. "Oh God, I'm sorry. That's not why I'm calling at all. I totally forgot, caller ID. It's Steph, Kerri's boss? You said I should call you to get together for coffee this week. I didn't even think about the fact that I was calling you from a work phone."

"Oh! Hey Steph! Sorry about that. It's just that the

phone has been ringing off the hook here all day with reporters looking for me to say something about the case now that the verdict has been read. I didn't mean to be rude."

"No, no, not at all. I should have realized. Does that mean you aren't interested in hanging out?" Steph started to feel a little weird about making the call to begin with.

"On the contrary. I think it is the perfect reason to get out of the house and let the machine say no comment for a while. Can I meet you at the Little Café in half an hour? I need to call my mom to come sit with Ava."

"That sounds great. I'll see you there in a bit." Steph put the receiver back in on the hook and sat at her desk to check her emails before she would head across the street to the coffee shop.

There were a few dozen emails waiting for her, nothing of real importance though. There were a couple of requests for time off, some press releases from the city that she knew would be handled by the municipal reporter and a few junk email offers from clothing stores. Steph closed the application and checked the time. Still 20 minutes before Summer would meet her. She shuffled the papers on her desk to tidy them a little and decided to head to the Little Café to wait.

There was a surprisingly long line for the middle of the afternoon on a weekday, but she had time to kill so she didn't mind. The woman behind the counter nodded as she saw Steph approach and without a word returned with an extra large coffee. Steph thanked her and found a table near the window where she could watch for Summer to arrive.

She smiled and stood from her seat as Summer approached, waving. Suddenly Steph was feeling self-conscious about the meeting and how she was supposed to act. She didn't have a lot of friends and found it hard to make them. It was much easier for her to just find herself with a friend group because of the person she was dating.

"Hey! Sorry I took so long but that's life with a little one. Gotta get someone to watch them every second of the day. You look like you are having quite the day yourself." Summer sat across from her.

Steph looked down, remembering that she had only thrown on sweats that morning and her normally perfect ponytail was in a weird bun on the top of her head. "I don't usually go out like this. It has been an interesting start to the day, for sure."

"I'm guessing that's why you called?" Summer smiled. "Seems like you could really use a friend to talk about it."

Steph took a deep breath and thought back on everything that had happened in the last 12 hours. It hadn't even been a full day since her and Julia went to dinner. It hadn't even been a full day since they slept together and now, she was fairly certain it was over. She could feel tears forming in the corners of her eyes and she sniffed to try to hold them back.

Summer reached across the table and placed her hand on Steph's arm. "Hey, it's okay. Whatever it is, I'm sure it will be alright."

"I'm sorry about this. I know we don't know each other very well and I really shouldn't put all of this on you, I just didn't know who else to talk to." She sighed. "You see, there is this girl…"

"There is always a girl," Summer joked. "I'm guessing you mean Julia? She seemed so smitten with you when I saw her the other day. What happened?"

"Well, things were going great I think, we were getting really close and then she spent the night last night and well…" Steph paused and cleared her throat.

"And…You don't have to get into the details, but that sounds like it is a good thing, not something to be upset about."

"It was a good thing, until this morning when my mother showed up without warning and found us in bed together," Steph's voice shook as she spoke and she showed vulnerability that she rarely allowed others to see.

Summer looked a little puzzled. "I'm not sure I understand. She didn't know you were dating?"

"She didn't know I am gay." Steph couldn't hold back the tears any longer. "She all but threw Julia out of the house, we had a screaming match and she slapped me. My mother has never raised a hand to me in my life and she slapped me. But that's not even the worst of it. I don't think Julia is going to forgive me."

Summer handed her a tissue from her purse and held her hand as Steph tried not to make it too obvious that she was crying in public. They sat in silence for a few minutes while Steph tried to collect herself.

"Have you tried talking to her?"

"I went to her place just after it happened. She said she needs time to think. I don't really know what that means. I know one thing, after today I will never again hide who I am. Not for anyone."

"Did you tell her that?" Summer squeezed Steph's arm.

"I tried. I just don't know if I got the message across the way I wanted to. I don't think I've ever felt like this about anyone and hiding that part of myself was something I wasn't willing to do anymore anyway. I was ready to come out to everyone if things worked out with Julia. I wanted to be able to walk around proud that she was a part of my life."

"Then give her the time. You know, I'm a lot like you. I found someone that I loved more than anything in this world, but I was so afraid of what it meant that I let her go. I broke her heart, and my own, because I was scared. I got lucky though." Summer held her left hand in front of her, fiddling with her engagement ring. "I got a second chance. I think, if you are patient and you give Julia the opportunity, she will come around and you can do it right."

"What about my mom? I said so many things to her this morning. I meant every word of what I said, but I shouldn't have shouted and been so cruel about it."

"Listen, I'm sure you weren't cruel, only honest. And sometimes the only way to get your point across is to shout. She is your mom, and she loves you. She may be hurting right now and unsure of how to grasp what happened, but she will come around." Summer smiled in reassurance.

"I'm not so sure. But to be honest, I'm just glad it is finally out in the open and I no longer have to hide."

"I know how you feel. There is nothing better than being able to share your whole self with the people you love."

"Well, I should get going. I'm sure it won't be long before I have to deal with my father, and I could use a shower and a change of clothes. Besides, you are probably eager to get back to Ava."

"Yeah, I should go. But Steph?" Summer stood and picked up her purse. "You can call me any time you need to talk, okay?"

"Thanks. And, same." Steph smiled.

CHAPTER 23

Steph had just stepped out of the shower when she heard a pounding at the front door. She wrapped herself in a towel and made her way to the porch. "Who is it?"

"Your father. Are you going to let me in?"

Steph swallowed hard. As if she hadn't had enough to deal with already that day, now she was going to have to hash things out with her dad. "It's unlocked. I just got out of the shower. Come on in, I'll be with you in a few minutes," She shouted as she made her way back to the bedroom.

When she emerged a few minutes later her father was still standing in the porch, picking through the mail she had left on the table and shaking his head. She watched and waited for him to notice her and speak, but he seemed enthralled with the latest building supply flyer.

"Hey Dad, so, what brings you to town?" Steph tried to play like she didn't know exactly why he was at her door.

"Pack a bag, you are coming home with me." His voice never wavered and sounded the same as it had when he would command her to put on a dress for church as a child.

"No," Was all Steph could reply through the lump in

her throat.

"I'm not asking you; I'm telling you. You are going to pack a bag and come home with me and your mother until we can find someone to help you with your sickness."

"No," She said again, firmer this time. "I'm not going to do any such thing. I'm not sick. I'm perfectly fine and I am not a child, so you can't keep treating me like one."

"As long as you live under my roof, I will treat you any way I please." He folded his arms across his chest. "And whether you like it or not, young lady, with my name on the papers, this is also my house. Now, gather some things together and get your butt out in the car before I have to force you."

Steph had always been a little afraid of her father. Not that he was abusive to her or her mother, but he had a temper, one that had seen him come home with a number of black eyes and bloody knuckles when Steph was a child. Her mother had already hit her that day and she wasn't keen to have her father do the same.

Steph's hands trembled as she balled her hands into fists and attempted to continue to stand her ground. "I have a life here, and a good job. I'm the chief editor at the paper for Christ's sake. I can't just pick up and go home with you because you don't like who I am dating." The trembling in her hands was making its way to her knees but she continued to stand firm.

Her father looked at her with a mix of distain and anger, his ears starting to turn pink as his blood pressure rose with each denial from her. "Okay, if that is how it is going to be, then so be it." He marched down the hall to her room.

Steph could hear the rustling as he pulled her gym bag from the closet and the sound of dresser drawers slamming as he searched through her things for items to pack. She couldn't help but have the same feeling she did on the day Nicole left. She was dragged back to the moment with the familiar sounds of the anger behind the slamming of the drawers and she once again found herself almost in tears thinking back to the moment that the relationship had ended. Steph quickly wiped her eyes so her father would not see that she was upset if he came back into the room. She braced herself and made her way down the hall after him.

"That is enough," She almost screamed as she saw the mess he had made of her room. Clothes were thrown all over the bed and the floor.

"Don't you have anything decent to wear? All these pantsuits and manly looking clothes and not one appropriate dress or lady's outfit. I don't know how I missed this happening to you or who did it, but I'm going to get you better, so if you aren't going to do this yourself, stay out of my way."

And then Steph did something she had never done in her life, she swore in front of her father. "Fuck this and fuck you. I will pack a bag, but it isn't because I'm leaving here with you. If you don't want me living truthfully under your roof, then I will find somewhere else to go." She grabbed the bag from his hands and started to pack the first items she laid her hands on. She knew she was probably going to regret her choices later, but she needed to do this fast and get away from the house.

"Excuse me, do you think you are going to talk to me like that and get away from me that easy?" Her father stood in the doorway, blocking her escape.

"I think you are going to move and let me go." Steph felt another surge of adrenaline flow through her causing her heart to beat so loud she could hear it in her ears. She walked toward him, standing almost nose to nose. "I may never have stood up to you in my life, I may have lived in fear of you finding out that I was gay since I was 17 years old, but today, today that all changes. I have nothing to fear anymore and there is nothing you can say or do to make me think that I do." She pushed her father aside and almost ran down the hall and out the front door.

Steph shivered immediately as a cool breeze blew around her, only in her shirt sleeves as she hadn't stopped for a coat, she also realized that she didn't even take her car keys. She hung her head and sighed, allowing some of the tension from the moment before to fall from her body. She looked back at the house to see if her father was following her, but only for a second before she threw the gym back over her shoulder and started to walk toward Main Street.

Steph wasn't sure where she was headed, only that it was away from her dad. She put her head down and scuffed her feet along the pavement continuing to move with no real sense of purpose or destination in mind when she looked up and found herself in front of the Observer office.

She did her best to avoid everyone as she made her way to her office to try to formulate a plan. She couldn't exactly live at the Observer, she couldn't afford a hotel, and she needed to find somewhere to sleep that night. Steph closed the door to her office and sat behind her desk to retrieve the list of apartments owned by the paper.

Steph knew that at least one of the apartments was still free after Kerri had moved out. She had been meaning to post it as available but with the stress of getting the mortgage on the house and the Closet Murderer case going to trial she had let it go by the wayside. Now, she was grateful that she had.

She picked up the phone and called the super of the building. "Hi there, it's Steph over at the Observer. I wanted to see how soon we could have an employee move into the vacant apartment."

A rough, brash voice replied, "Well, could be a couple of days. Haven't had the chance to get in there and do a thorough clean since the last one moved out."

Steph's shoulders sagged at the news. She would still have to worry about at least two nights that she didn't feel like she could go home. If this had happened just yesterday, she was certain she would have immediately called Julia. Now, she wasn't sure where to turn. "I suppose that will be okay." Any chance it could be ready before the weekend?"

"I doubt it. We can shampoo the carpets this afternoon, but that is going to be at least a couple of days to dry. Is it urgent?"

"Somewhat. I have, ah, a reporter who needs somewhere to stay, short term, as soon as possible."

"Well, I can give you the keys tomorrow, but I wouldn't recommend anyone moving in until at least Sunday." The gruff voice coughed.

"Okay. That should be fine. I'll come by for the keys at lunch tomorrow."

"See you then," Was all that was said before there was a click in the receiver and Steph heard nothing more but a dial tone.

Steph dropped the receiver and buried her face in her hands, no longer willing to hold back the tears. Her shoulders heaved with every breath as she finally let everything that happened that day wash over her. She could hardly believe that her whole life could be turned upside down so quickly. Her parents hated her, Julia didn't want to speak to her, and she had nowhere to go. It certainly wasn't the way she thought this day would go when she woke up that morning.

Steph knew that even though she was finally looking back on what had happened, it was going to take some time before it all truly sank in. She had been crying so long that her throat was starting to hurt from holding back loud sobs.

There was a sudden knock at her door and she quickly grabbed a tissue from her desk and tried to wipe away the tears before she replied. "Come in." She cleared her throat after hearing the thickness of her voice and forced a smile for whoever was about to enter.

Kerri popped her head around the door frame with a concerned look. "Hey! What are you doing here? I thought this was your day off. There can't be anything so important that you had to come in this afternoon, is there?"

Steph tried to speak but she could only shake her head for fear the tears would start again. She motioned for Kerri to enter and pointed at the chair in front of her, clearing her throat again to try to force the words to come. "It's just been a bit of a rough day."

Kerri flopped into the seat across from Steph, the look of concern on her face growing. "Do you want to talk about it?"

"Actually, I talked to Summer about some of it earlier, but things have just gotten worse. I don't know if I really want to get into the details right now." Steph bowed her head.

"That's okay. You don't have to tell me anything if you don't want to." Kerri glanced around the office, noticing the gym bag in the corner for the first time. "Are you planning a trip?"

Steph could no longer stop herself from crying. "No, not really. I just can't go home right now. Long story short, I had a huge fight with my parents and now they want to send me to some sort of conversion camp and my dad says the house is as much his as it is mine so unless I give in to what they want, I'm no longer welcome there."

"Wow. You are having a rough day. So, what does that mean? Do you have somewhere to stay? I don't think that chair is a great place to sleep." Kerri pointed at her office seat.

Steph shook her head. "The apartment you were renting is vacant, but they are in the process of cleaning it, so I can move in there in a couple of days. I don't really have a plan of what I'm going to do until then," She choked.

"What about Julia? Things seemed like they were going well with you two. Could you ask to stay with her until the place is ready?"

"That would be a no. She is pretty mad at me right now and I don't know if she will ever want to see me again, never mind have me living with her for even a couple of days." Steph grabbed another tissue and wiped her cheeks and nose.

"Okay. Well, I guess that means you are coming to stay with me and Summer." Kerri stood from the seat.

"I can't intrude on you guys like that. I mean, you just got engaged. You don't need a third wheel kicking around the house right now, even if it is just for the weekend."

"Don't be silly. We have the rest of our lives to be just the two of us...well, and Ava, but you're my friend and you need us. I'll call Summer right now and tell her that we need to make up the guest room." Kerri moved toward the door. "I don't want to hear another thing about it. You'll stay with us for as long as you need."

Steph just nodded; her jaw dropped at the way Kerri had commanded her. "Okay. Thanks."

"Grab your bag and head over to the house. Summer's mother, Joan, is there watching Ava. I'll let her know you are on the way." Kerri opened the door to the office and waited for Steph to move from the desk. "Go on, there is no need for you to be here when you are this upset."

"Okay. Will do." Steph picked up her bag and followed Kerri to the door. "I don't know what else to say, but thank you."

"It's no problem at all. I'll see you later tonight and you can tell me all about it if you like. Or not. It's up to you." Kerri ushered Steph down the hall and out of the building.

CHAPTER 24

Steph was seated at the dining room table with Joan and Summer, drinking a glass of wine, which was honestly her third, when Kerri walked through the door. She smiled as best as she was able and waved as Kerri crossed the house to join them.

"Six thirty and we are already getting into the hard stuff I see," Kerri laughed.

"Well, mostly me. Although these lovely ladies were nice enough to at least poor themselves a drop and pretend to join me." Steph's smile was a little less forced now. She could already feel the glow that drinking wine always gave her.

Summer laughed and took a deep swallow from her glass. "I'm not pretending anything, I just didn't want to drink too fast and be half in the bag by the time Kerri got home. I'm pretty much a lightweight these days."

Joan laughed and finished her glass. "That you are, my girl. But you always were." She stood from the table and brushed the wrinkles from her pants. "Well, I suppose I will get home and leave you ladies to chat." She placed her hand gently on Steph's shoulder. "Take it from a Mom. No matter what is happening right now, or how mad your parents seem to be, they will get past it because they are going to realize they love you more than anything and they want you to be a part of their lives, no matter what."

Steph placed her hand over Joan's and looked up at the soft smile she was offering. "Thanks Mrs. Donnelly. I can't say that I believe you right now, but I hope you are right." She let her hand slide back down into her lap and sighed deeply as Joan patted her shoulder and headed toward the door.

"Well, I suppose I will get you ladies a refill." Kerri marched into the kitchen and returned with a glass of whiskey for herself and the bottle of wine, carefully pouring a third of the bottle into each glass.

"If I didn't know better, I would say you were trying to get me drunk," Summer teased, in an attempt to lighten the mood.

Steph chuckled despite herself and raised her glass to the table. "To people that I didn't know would be good friends just 24 hours ago."

Kerri and Summer exchanged a look of agreement they were doing the right thing and connected their glasses to the one Steph had raised.

"I'm really sorry for what you are going through. I wish there was more I could do to help." Kerri bowed her head and peered at the ice that she rattled around in her glass.

"You have no idea how much this means to me, just having a place to go right now and to know that I'm with people who understand what I'm going through makes it even better." Steph was starting to slur a little and knew that if she continued on this train, she was going to be a drunk crying mess in no time. "But enough about that, let's talk about something happier. I believe you two have a wedding to plan!"

Kerri couldn't help but smile at the mention of the upcoming event. "I suppose we do, but we don't have to think about that now. Tonight is all about you."

"Well, I think the best thing we can do for me is help me think about anything else. So, tell me all about the big day." Steph forced a smile. She was very good at compartmentalizing her feelings and needed to do just that.

Summer squealed with glee, "So, we have the place picked out and I put a deposit down last week so one of the big things is already taken care of."

"I suppose you have some big fancy hall." Steph smiled, more naturally this time.

"Nope. We decided to get married back in Jenkinstown, where we first met and that the most appropriate place would be Willie's Bar of all things. They have a great room in the back because it used to be a restaurant, so we booked that. It's not going to be a huge event or anything. I mean, I already did this once and it was a disaster, so Kerri agreed that we could just do something small and simple."

Kerri stood behind Summer, grasping her shoulders. "I never thought I would actually get married, so doing this at all is enough for me. I don't need some big fancy affair."

"That's great, you guys." Steph leaned back in her chair, swirling the wine in her glass as she watched the way Summer and Kerri were interacting. "You seem so, so happy. But tell me more!"

"We are in high planning mode because we only have two months until the big day." Kerri shook Summer gently in her chair, "I let this one get away once, and I don't want to give her time to change her mind this time," She chuckled.

"Now, you know that is never going to happen." Summer reached back and poked Kerri in the side, causing her to grunt and buckle over. "I didn't get you that hard, stop being so foolish." She shook her head.

"That's a really short timeline. But you know what, why wait, right?" Steph's mind drifted back to one of the many times Nicole had brought up the idea of marriage.

"You know, I think it might be time for you to make an honest woman out of me." Nicole was lying naked beside her in the bed and gently stroking Steph's neck with her fingertips.

"Is that right?" She said, in a joking tone. "You think that just because I give you pleasure that you had never experienced before I should have to go out and throw away thousands of dollars on a ring, then spend thousands and thousands more on a party, just so you can feel like an honest woman?" Steph kissed her on the top of the head. "Tell me, how do you think that makes any sense, and what's wrong with how things are right now?" She looked down at Nicole and could immediately tell that she wasn't in on the joke.

"I just think it's time for us to take the next step, is all." Nicole pouted, pulling away slightly from Steph's embrace.

"I've told you," Steph pulled her back in, "I have a five-year plan. Once everything falls into place, then we can talk about this."

"Yeah, yeah. The five-year plan. This is year three, Steph. When you first started talking about this five-year plan, I figured we would at least be engaged by now and married by the end of the five years. I didn't know that you meant you wanted to wait five years before you even considered the idea."

"I guess I should have been more clear then." Steph pulled away and sat on the edge of the bed, searching for her clothes.

Nicole pulled the blankets up over her chest and sighed.

"I'm sorry I brought it up."

"Yeah, me too." Steph pulled on her shorts and grabbed a t-shirt, slipping it over her arms as she walked out of the room.

"So, it's just to finish making the invitations and we are all set," Summer finished as Steph drifted back into reality.

"Hmm? Oh, that's great! I'm always around to help if you need anything." Steph tried not to let them know that she hadn't been listening. She picked up her cell phone for what felt like the thousandth time and checked to see if she had any messages or missed calls. Steph had a bad habit of leaving her phone on silent or vibrate so it didn't disturb her at work and although she knew she had turned the ringer on that evening, she still couldn't help but look.

Kerri gave her a knowing glance, "Why don't you call her?" She sat down at the end of the table, pouring herself another glass of whiskey.

"She said she needed time, and I plan to give it to her. I just kind of thought she might have at least texted to see if I was okay after today, to let me know that she is. I mean, I know this morning was awful, but we always said we were friends, first and foremost."

"She's hurting. You're hurting. But I'm sure she is fine and besides, you will see her at work in the morning," Summer added.

"I wish I could say that was a good thing. It's like my worst fear about all of this is coming true. We wanted it so much that we looked past the problems for just long enough that now we are fighting, and I still have to be her boss and she still has to see and deal with me every day. What if we can't get past this?"

Kerri sighed and looked at Summer for support.

"Trust me, if we can get past everything that we have been through and get to where we are now, you will too. I can't promise that Julia will ever really get over what happened and that it will be sunshine and roses, but I can promise that you will both find a way to keep working together and at the very least, keep being friends."

They sat in silence for a few minutes, no one really knowing what to say when Kerri's phone started to ring from the kitchen and she quickly got up to answer it. "It's probably just Jack, wondering if I decided on the tie colours for our tuxes yet. I'll be right back."

Summer nodded and leaned back in her chair. "Kerri's brother."

Steph raised an eyebrow, "What?"

"Jack, its Kerri's brother. I think he might be even more invested in our relationship than we are at this point. God love him, he was always so supportive of the two of us together. Kerri asked him to be her best man."

Steph just nodded along as Summer spoke, unsure of how to join in the conversation and straining to hear the conversation in the kitchen. "That's great. It's really nice that she has a brother that cares so much about her happiness."

"What about you? Do you have any siblings?" Summer tried to engage her.

"Uh, yeah. Two sisters, but we aren't close. The oldest one, Sherri, got married right after high school, to the captain of the hockey team, no less, and settled down just a block from my parents. I could never understand her and why she didn't want more from life than to stay in the town where she grew up and pop out babies for a living rather than go to school and make something of herself. I didn't get to know her all that well because she was six years older than me and was married by the time I was a teenager."

"And the other?" Summer pushed, as she realized Steph was finally thinking about something other than Julia.

"The other. Well, people used to call Jane the black sheep of the family, but I suppose I get that title now. She was always a little different, making her own style, reading philosophy and a lot of Sylvia Plath. Middle child stuff, you know? She listened to music that most people in town had never heard of and she refused to go to church with the family. She is only two years older than me, so we grew up together, but when she turned 15, she suddenly wanted nothing to do with her baby sister tagging along behind her everywhere she went. When she graduated she moved out west for school and we didn't really keep in touch. Is that a terrible thing?" Steph rarely talked about her family at all, and even less about her sisters.

"It's not terrible. Not all siblings are close, I suppose. I can't really say much on the subject, to be honest, being an only child and all."

"That sounds like a joy. There were so many times I wished I was an only child. But, then again, I only got away with some of the things I did as a kid because I had siblings that took up more of the attention. No one notices you as much when you are the youngest. My parents doted over my oldest sister and spent the rest of their time focused on trying to keep the other one out of trouble. I could get away with almost anything, including keeping the fact that I was gay a secret. Well, until now anyway." Steph put her hands over her face, rubbed across her forehead and down her cheeks until her hands were in a prayer position under her chin.

"I understand, you know. I kept it a secret for a long time too. I was even so ashamed of it that I went as far as to try to pretend to be straight for more years than I want to remember. Christ, I even got married and had a baby to try to convince myself and everyone else that it was true." Summer bowed her head as Kerri returned, placing her hand on her shoulder. "Jack?"

"Not Jack." Kerri shook her head, her voice rising as she spoke. "Julia."

Steph perked up at the mention of the name. Her eyes widened and she was now on the edge of her seat waiting to hear more. "She okay?" She moved her hands, still in prayer position in front of her lips.

"She's okay." Kerri smiled. "She says she will talk to you tomorrow, but she just needed to vent to someone tonight."

Steph sighed with relief for the first time in what felt like days and slouched back in the chair. "Well, on that note, I suppose I should go to bed. It's an early start tomorrow." She pulled herself up from the table and walked toward the stairs that led to the second story bedrooms. "Thanks again for taking me in."

"Anytime." Summer was at her heals and shooed her to continue to the room. "Get some sleep. We'll chat more tomorrow."

Steph closed the door to the room, flopped backwards on the bed and closed her eyes, grateful for the wine that would put her into a deep sleep that night.

CHAPTER 25

It was quiet in the Observer office when Steph arrived the next morning. This wasn't unusual as she often arrived long before most of the morning staff, but it felt strange and eerie on this particular day. Steph shuddered and tried to push the feeling away as she cautiously opened the door to her office and glanced around like a child checking for monsters under the bed. She wasn't sure what she expected to find, but she had a strange feeling that someone or something was waiting for her.

Steph sighed in relief at the empty office and flopped into her chair, dropping her bag on the floor and started shuffling through the stack of mail that was placed on her desk. Steph always felt like she was playing catch up at work, and it was even more apparent after a day off.

She picked up the national paper that arrived earlier that morning and found herself enthralled with an article about the mortgage crisis, and how the housing bubble had burst, sending a number of major mortgage companies into bankruptcy. She was so captivated by the piece that she didn't hear the door to her office open and nearly jumped out of her chair when Julia cleared her throat to announce her presence.

"Sorry, I didn't mean to startle you. That must be some

story." Julia gestured at the paper that was now lying over Steph's computer keyboard.

"It's crazy, what is happening with all the people defaulting on their mortgage right now. Just think, if I could have only waited a few more months I probably never would have needed my father's help to buy the house." Steph shook her head, wanting to say more, to say that it would have meant that they wouldn't be fighting right now, that she would still feel nothing but blissful when she saw Julia's face and not the panic that she was feeling at this moment.

"Yeah, and then maybe yesterday never would have happened," Julia said the words for her. "Actually, I came to see if you had a few minutes to talk about it some more."

"Sure. Close the door." Steph folded the paper and took a deep breath while she waited for Julia to sit. "No matter how many times I go over it in my head, I don't know what to say that will make any of this better."

"How about I talk, and you listen?" Julia crossed foot over her knee and ran her hands over her thighs.

"I can do that."

"I want to start with the positive. First of all, I'm glad you are out to your parents. It isn't the way I would have liked to see it happen for you, but I'm glad it finally did. I don't know if we could have worked if you did the same thing to me that you did to Nicole. I'm not ashamed of who I am and I'm only with someone if I am proud to say that I am and I want my person to feel that way too."

"I could never be ashamed of you, I..." Steph started to interject.

Julia raised her index finger to her lips and made a shushing sound. "I talk, remember?"

Steph blushed with embarrassment and nodded sheepishly in response.

"Okay. So, I feel like step one is out of the way, but if you want to really try to make this work with me, you need to be out, all the way out. That means I want to be able to tell people I'm dating you without having to worry if they are someone who doesn't know. It means that I want to be able to slow dance with you at a party and hold hands and make gooey eyes over our table at the café. It means no shaking my hand away if we are walking down the street and you see someone you know. Do you understand what I'm saying?" Julia waited for Steph to reply. "You can speak now."

Steph let out a breath she didn't realize she had been holding in and started to stammer, "I understand, but you need to know that I didn't really keep it from anyone I was close to besides my family and I only ever backed away from public affection because I was afraid it would somehow get back to them." Steph took another deep breath, looking at Julia for permission to continue.

"I'm going to need more than excuses for your past behaviour." Julia folded her arms across her chest.

"The other reason I don't like people to know has nothing to do with my crazy religious family, and more to do with my career." Steph paused.

"Why would who you sleep with have anything to do with your job?"

"Well, I'm pretty sure I was fired from my first placement out of school because of it." Steph could feel a lump forming in her throat.

"You got fired from a job? I don't believe it," Julia shot back.

"I've never really talked about it and I don't even put

it on my resume since I started here. It was the final weeks of classes and I was actually recruited to start as a senior reporter for a small-town paper a couple of states over. I was there a month and things seemed to be going really well. I was getting great feedback from my boss and being offered bigger and bigger opportunities in a very short time. That's when I started dating Valerie.

"She was absolutely gorgeous and way out of my league, so I couldn't believe my luck when she agreed to go out with me. We were only together a couple of weeks when my boss called me into his office and started shouting at me about morality and how much a journalist can impact a community. I don't really remember most of what he said, but the punchline was to pack my desk and leave," Steph finished and wiped a tear from her cheek.

Julia unfolded her arms and leaned forward in her chair. "I'm sorry. I had no idea. But you know that times have changed, this isn't some small hick town and that you are the boss now, right?"

"I know that," Steph sobbed. "That is what I kept telling Nicole that I was waiting for. If I was the boss, it didn't matter if anyone found out. Sorry, I don't mean to keep bringing her up. It's just that it feels like the fight I have been having for the last five years with her is the same fight that we are living right now."

"It's okay to bring her up. I would never ask you to stop talking about someone or something that was such a big part of your life for so long. What I am asking is that you stop hiding and until you do, we are through." Julia stood and turned toward the door.

Steph couldn't speak. She just nodded and watched as Julia left, closing the door behind her. It was going to be a long day and she still had to find time to go back to her house and pick more clothes for the week. In her haste to leave she had thrown mostly sweats in the bag and she certainly couldn't show up to work with Juicy printed on her ass.

Steph shuffled the papers around on her desk, trying to force herself to start working, but to no avail. This might be one of the times when she wasn't able to keep her feelings in a little box anymore and they could easily come spilling out for the world to see. That would be her worst nightmare. She sighed heavily and decided she would take her morning break early and head to the house for clothes and hopefully, her car.

It was a long, brisk walk from the office to her home, about 20 blocks and the air felt more like fall than she had expected. She was pleased to see the only car in her driveway was her own, which she hoped meant her parents had headed home after their fight the day before. Steph took a deep breath before opening the door to the house and quietly stepped inside. She jumped with fright as she found her mother and their minister sitting on her couch.

"What in the name of God are you doing here?" Steph said without thinking. "Sorry, Father. I mean, why are you here?"

"It's okay, my child. Your mother says you have the devil in you and that you needed someone from the church to come and help you get back on the path to heaven."

"Did she now?" Steph glared at her mother who sat with her hands folded in her lap as though she was at a church service. She turned to the priest who couldn't have been more than a couple of years out of the seminary. "What exactly did she tell you?"

"She said you had fallen off the Godly path and were making choices in your life that were putting you on the path to hell and that only my guidance could get you back on track." The priest adjusted his white collar.

"I think she has wasted your time, Father. I don't have any plans to try and pray the gay away now, or in the future." Steph turned and pointed her finger at her mother. "If this is some kind of conversion therapy joke, it isn't funny."

"It isn't a joke, honey. I just want my little girl to meet me at the gates with Jesus and I know that if you don't change you are going to find yourself in hell for eternity."

"I hope I do," Steph clapped back. "If being gay means going to hell, then at least I will be with friends." She turned her attention to the priest. "And as for you, they banned conversion therapy in these parts years ago and I would think a young man of the church like yourself would have more liberal ideas than to think you can change a person's sexuality with prayer."

"I…ah…" he stammered back, "I didn't know your sexuality had anything to do with it." He choked on the words and glanced between the mother and daughter on either side of him. "You are right, Stephanie. This is not the place for the church to try and intervene. This is a family matter. If you need guidance with communication and working through this struggle as a family, I will be here to listen, as will God." He stood from the couch and made his way to the door.

"Father, wait. You need to help my daughter before it's too late." Steph's mother chased after him.

The priest took her hands in his and looked into her eyes as he spoke. "Listen to your child. Find the common ground. Remember the love you share and that although you found something about her that you don't like, don't let it be stronger than the bond between a mother and child." He dropped her hands and left.

"How dare he!" Her mother shouted at the door before huffing her way back to the couch. "What am I supposed to do about you now?"

"Mom, you need to take his advice and listen to me," Steph stated in her professional voice, without meaning to. "You need to understand that it is okay that I'm gay."

"Never. I will never accept that." She folded her arms like a petulant child and flopped back on the couch in the same way. "There has to be something I can do to change you, save your soul."

"Mom," Steph started again, sitting beside her, "You can't change this. I can't change this. God knows that I tried when I was younger to not be, but I was kidding myself. I was depressed and unhappy and there was even a point where I considered killing myself over it."

At the mention of suicide her mother's eyes widened and she sat up straight. "Well that would have also meant you were going to hell," Her voice softened slightly. "You wouldn't really do something like that, would you Stephy?"

"No, not anymore. But it's because I stopped trying to pretend to be what I thought the world wanted me to be and just started to live my life in a way that made me happy. It was a lot of secrets from a lot of people, which is hard, but I learned how to love myself anyway and how, in turn, to love someone else." Steph paused, deciding how much she really wanted to tell her mother. "All of that happened, I stopped being sad and withdrawn and it was all because I met Nicole."

"You were, I mean, I guess I should have realized after I found out, but you two were, together?"

"Yes. Happily, for the last five years. We made life plans together, we put each other in our futures, but I refused to tell you about her. I refused to tell anyone, really, and she left me."

"I don't want to hear any more of this. No matter what you say, it wasn't a real relationship and you can't convince me otherwise. It was a delusion that you constructed that will never be recognized by God. And she is out of the picture now, so this is my chance to make you normal again. The beautiful little girl that I raised." She reached out her hand to touch Steph's face, but Steph pushed it away.

"You know what, I'm sure you believe that. I'm sure that you can't see past what you think is normal enough to realize that it was real. It was more real than a lot of straight relationships out there because we were only together for ourselves and each other." Steph's brow furrowed as she looked at her mother for a reaction. "And now, I've met someone else. Someone that I could truly love, but I don't know if any of that is possible now, after what happened."

Her mother snapped her fingers and sat up to the edge of the couch. "I'll find you a nice boy. I know there are a couple around with some nice feminine qualities that you might like. Some of them are so dirty and gross, but there has to be one out there that will suit your needs."

"It doesn't matter how clean they are, or well-dressed or anything like that. It will still be a guy and I will still be gay." Steph grabbed her forehead and grunted with anger.

"But God…"

"Why can't you see that God wants me to be happy?" Steph realized she was pacing and shouting. She stopped to calm her voice. She already felt like she might as well be arguing with a vacuum. "Doesn't your bible preach that Jesus loves all of his children and that we should likewise all love each other?"

"Yes, but…"

"So, where does it have the footnote that 'this does not include certain races, religions or sexualities?' Is there somewhere that it says you can't learn to accept me for who I am, regardless of who I sleep with?"

Her mother sat in silence, and for the first time in their whole conversation Steph felt like she was getting through to her. She watched as her mother searched for something to say to come back at her.

"Mom? Do you love me?"

"Of course I do, honey, I just don't love this choice for you. I could never stop loving you."

"Then you are going to need to learn to love all of me and to accept the person that I eventually decide to spend my life with, even though it will be a woman." Steph fell into the matching chair next to the sofa and leaned her elbows on her knees. "I know this has all been very upsetting for you, but please, try. Here." Steph pulled a card from her pocket and handed it to her mother.

"What's this supposed to be?" She turned the card over in her hands. "Parents and friends of lesbians and gays? Why are you giving me this?"

"I want you and Dad to go to a meeting. Just go, talk to the people there. They have all been through what you are going through right now and I think it will really help you to understand me and that it could make this okay."

"Nothing anyone can say or do is going to make this okay with me. I will talk to your father about the house, though, as long as you promise not to bring any of your little friends around. I can't have you living on the streets."

"You don't have to worry about me. I have somewhere

to stay. If you want to do something for me, go to the meeting." Steph pulled herself from the chair and made her way toward the bedroom. "Now, if you'll excuse me, I have to get some clothes and get back to work."

***

At the end of the day, Steph pulled into the driveway at Kerri and Summer's place and laid her head on the steering wheel. To say that she had lived the most emotionally draining 48 hours of her life was an understatement and she wasn't ready to make small talk. She clicked the key back in the car to turn on the radio and leaned back in the seat.

There was a tapping on the window beside her and Steph suddenly realized she was cold and it was much darker than when she had arrived. She opened her eyes to find Summer standing at the window with a sweater wrapped around her and a concerned look on her face.

Steph turned off the car and opened the driver side door to exit, shivering in the wind as she did. She quickly grabbed an armful of clothes from the backseat and followed Summer into the house.

"Sorry if I disturbed you, it was just getting pretty cold and I didn't want you to freeze." Summer took some of the items from Steph's arms and carried them up the stairs to the guest room.

"No, it's okay. I hadn't meant to be out there so long. I just wanted to take a minute to decompress and that apparently turned into an hour. It's just been a lot to deal with over the last couple of days and I'm pretty tired."

"I can imagine. Why don't you just lie down and get some rest? We can talk about it tomorrow night, if you like." Summer smiled, and waited for Steph to nod before leaving her.

CHAPTER 26

By the time Steph got to work the next morning, she had made an important decision. She was going to come out to the staff, she just wasn't sure how she wanted to go about it. Steph thought about casually mentioning it to one or two people and waiting for the rumour to circulate, but she was afraid if she didn't pick the right people no one would find out or that it would take too long and she would be dealing with it for weeks instead of all at once.

Steph also wanted to make the gesture enough to get Julia's attention and let her know that she was serious about wanting a relationship. It had to be something that really said 'I'm out and proud and I want you all at once.' Steph checked her calendar to make sure she didn't have anything important happening that morning before sitting down to try to devise a plan. There was nothing scheduled for that day, but Steph did remind herself of the full staff meeting later in the week.

Then, as though an actual lightbulb had appeared above her head, she knew what she was going to do. Steph grabbed a note pad and started to scribble the way she would in short hand at a press conference. She started to smile, genuinely, for what felt like the first time in forever, as she forced her hand to move faster across the page. Within a few minutes she was finished. She slapped the book down on the desk and sat back in her chair, satisfied.

***

The day of the meeting Steph was also moving into the apartment next to the offices. It didn't take long that morning as she only had a couple of bags of clothing at Summer and Kerri's and she didn't plan to go back to her house until she had given her parents more time to cool down, especially after what happened the last time.

Steph put on her favourite pants suit and her flashy red Adidas sneakers, checked her ponytail one more time and took a deep breath before leaving for work. She was about to do something that she never thought she would consider in her life and the mix of fear and excitement was overwhelming.

As she made her way through the doors a number of people were standing around and she found herself almost giggling as she greeted them. Steph noticed a few giving her strange looks, but she brushed it off and continued to her office, closing the door behind her.

It was still an hour before she would find her pack of reporters gathered in the conference room for the first time since it was announced that she would be taking over as the editor-in-chief. That meeting felt like an eternity ago, even though it had only been a couple of months. She knew the job would change her and her life, but Steph never could have predicted the crazy things that would have happened since then.

She attempted to distract herself by checking emails and sending out story ideas for the senior reporters to investigate, but she mostly found herself tapping her pen against the desk and counting down the minutes, or pacing around the room and going over what she planned to say. It would be all the usual quarterly update stuff, of course, but no one would be expecting the end of her speech.

Steph opened her door and peeked out to see if people had started to gather. She could hear laughter coming down the hall and many office doors around her opening with heavy foot falls making their way to the meeting. She waited until it seemed like everyone had been seated around the table before making her way into the room.

Steph stood as firmly as she could, the papers in her hands shaking so much she could hardly read them. She forced her voice to steady as she went over the awards they had recently won and waited patiently as reporters whooped and hollered and congratulated each other. She was coming to the end of the official meeting and she also knew that some of the junior reporters were starting to get restless. She looked over to the side of the room where they had all congregated in hopes of getting a glimpse of Julia before she continued.

"Finally, something that was not included on the agenda for the quarterly today." Steph swallowed hard, and breathed slowly, grasping for every ounce of bravery and courage she could muster. "In fact, I have something to say of a personal nature. Something that I just want to get out in the open."

Steph looked around the room as many stared back at her confused, but others just seemed to be nodding along. She wasn't sure if it was because they had some idea of what she was going to say or if they just weren't really paying attention. Some part of her hoped it was because they already knew. When she made eye contact with Julia, however, she realized that was probably not the case as the person who had asked her to do this looked just as confused as most of the others.

Steph's chest shook with every breath as she forced herself to continue, "As you all know I have always been the type to keep my personal life very, very private, and, as some of you may have guessed, or even started rumours about in the early days of my career here, I do that because I am gay." She stopped letting the word land on the rest of the room like a bomb.

Steph watched as even those that had not been paying attention were now perked and at the ready to hear the rest of what she had to say. "For a long time I was in a relationship with someone that I refused to bring to gatherings with all of you, that I refused to take home to meet my parents, and that I pushed away because of it. Questions?" Steph startled herself, she hadn't meant to open the floor for people to ask more about her life.

Julia cleared her throat from the back of the room, "I have a few," she said matter of factly, her eyes wide and intense.

Steph chuckled nervously, "okay, shoot."

"So, what you are saying is that you are trying not to relive your past mistakes?"

"That's right."

"And you are saying that going forward you are going to be living your life open and honestly with those around you? All of those around you?" Julia's questions were getting more intense and she was slowly moving across the room to where Steph was standing.

"I am."

"So, you're telling me…ah…all of us, that you aren't going to keep your relationships a secret anymore and you plan to be out and proud about whomever you are dating?"

"Correct again. Anything else?" Steph asked, looking deeply into Julia's eyes as she now stood directly in front of her.

"Is there a reason you are coming out now?"

"Yes. After I pushed away my last girlfriend by keeping her in the closet, I recently met someone new and I don't want to see that happen with her. So, I'm standing before you, getting this all out in the open with the hope that I won't put her through that and I won't find myself hurt again because I am afraid." Steph stopped and looked around the room at the dozens of captivated faces she had forgotten were still there.

Julia took a step back and raised her pencil in the air, "One final question, if you don't mind?"

"I...I guess so." Steph kept one eye on Julia and one on the room, waiting to see if people were whispering about the news.

"What are you doing on Friday night?" Julia smiled and bit her lower lip.

"Well, I'm sorry to say that I have plans that night." Steph smiled and closed the gap between their bodies. "I believe I have a date with you."

With that statement, Julia grabbed the lapel of Steph's jacket and pulled her into a kiss, causing the room to erupt with applause. She released her and stared at Julia who grinned wryly and whispered in her ear, "See, nothing to be afraid of." She kissed her again and the room around them was now a buzz of conversation and congratulations.

Steph turned out of the moment as people started to stand and move toward them. She shook hands with a number of reporters who wanted to say how happy they were for them, and even a few that made a point of talking about the tension between the pair around the office.

There were a few who had figured out why, but for the most part, they were just relieved that it wasn't a work issue.

Steph felt a little bit more weight lift from her shoulders with every person she spoke to. They were accepting her, not pushing her away and not just accepting, they were happy for her. They were embracing her chance at happiness the same way she was finally trying to do.

As the crowd started to filter out of the conference room and back to work Steph snuck back to her office to catch her breath and enjoy the response she received. She closed the door and leaned against it, holding it shut and laughing to herself.

"How long have I been holding back in every moment of life that I feel this elated to just say it?" She spoke aloud to herself. She wanted to jump up and down and dance and scream all in the same moment. Not only could she put aside much of the fear she had been feeling, Julia agreed to see her again. She was still leaning against the door when she heard a soft knock. She turned around, startled at the sound and opened the door quickly.

"Well, that was a turn of events I was not expecting this morning." Kerri stood before her in the doorway.

"To be honest, I started thinking about what I would say a few days ago, but I only really decided when I stood in the room to go through with it. I just knew that Summer was right. If I wanted to get Julia to understand that I was serious about being out and about being with her, I had to make a big gesture, and fast."

"Well, that was certainly a big gesture. I'm happy for you." Kerri smiled and leaned against the doorframe. "And I know things with work out with your folks, too. They just need a little time."

Steph bowed her head. "I hope you're right."

CHAPTER 27

After three months of living in the Observer owned apartment, Steph was finally packing her bags to move back into her home. The apartment felt empty as she made her way to the door, even though the only thing she owned in it was her clothes. Her life had changed so dramatically in the time she spent in this place.

"Why do you look so sad?" Julia brushed aside Steph's ponytail and pressed her lips lightly to the back of her neck.

Steph shivered at the touch and smiled. "Because being in the place brought us together. If it hadn't been for that day with my mom, I'm not sure we would be having this conversation."

"Well, no. You never would have been forced to move out of your own house," Julia chuckled at her own bad joke. "But things are looking up."

"Things have been going so well for us here. I just don't want that big house and inviting my parents back into my life to change any of it." Steph turned to face Julia in the doorway, slipping her arms over her shoulders.

"Oh, honey. It's not going to. I have been right beside you, watching every step of the way as they made the effort to make things better between you. They reached out to you, they called and yelled and talked everything through. You didn't. You stood your ground, so this move is a big step forward in their understanding."

"I'm still not sure. I mean, after all this time, you still haven't actually met them."

"I would like to say something about that, but the truth is, we haven't been dating that long so there was no reason for us to have a proper introduction before this. I suppose I did kind of meet your mom that one time." She laughed. "Meeting the parents is a big deal." Julia squeezed her hands around Steph's hips. "I am, however, willing. That is, if they are."

"I could set something up. I mean, I would feel a lot better about their efforts if they would be willing to meet you." Steph smiled.

"Then it is settled. Let's get you moved home and we can see when they are free." Julia grabbed the gym bag from beside Steph's feet and headed down the hall toward the elevator.

Steph sighed and took one last look at the apartment before closing the door and following her. She was already nervous about calling her mom, but this was a big step forward in her relationship with Julia and one that she had to take.

***

A few days later Steph was finally settled back in at her house and it felt like Julia had been there since she moved in. They were sitting on the couch, watching Buffy for what seemed like the thousandth time to Steph when the phone rang. Steph paused the show, grateful for a break. As much as she loved spending time with Julia and doing the things that she liked, she wished Julia would get some new interests, or at least find a new show that she liked. "That does it, I'm getting cable." She shouted over her shoulder to Julia as she made her way to the kitchen to answer the phone.

"Hello," Steph answered casually. She was already fairly sure who would be on the other end of the line as most people would have called her cell phone.

"Hi Stephy," her mom replied cheerily. "I got your message. You wanted to talk?"

Steph swallowed hard. "I know we have been getting along better in the last couple of months, and I think it is time that you officially met my..." She paused unsure, "Julia."

"You're right. With all the time that you are spending with that girlfriend of yours, it's high time you bring her home to meet the family."

Steph couldn't reply. Her mom had called Julia her girlfriend without even a second of hesitation.

"Are you still there?" Her mother offered after a few minutes of silence.

"Yes. Still here. What do you mean by the family?"

"I wasn't going to say anything, I wanted it to be a surprise, but your sister is coming home for a couple of weeks. She gets here on Saturday, so I was hoping you would both like to come for Sunday dinner."

Steph sat down in a flop at the kitchen table. She was expecting pushback from her mom, not this. Maybe she really had underestimated how much her parent's opinion had changed in the last few months. She hadn't actually spoken to either of her sisters since her parents found out she was gay, but she assumed her mother had told them.

"Gee, you are awful silent this evening. Would you

like to bring Julia for supper on Sunday or not?"

"Will everyone be okay with that?" Steph replied, scratching the back of her neck nervously.

"Of course they will. I told you, your father and I went to see that priest about counseling and it made me see that there is nothing wrong with you. Sure, your father is even out at one of those PFLAG meetings right now. I usually go with him, but it is some sort of planning committee for this year's pride celebration. I swear, he is going to have that group taken over before too long."

"Dad is at a PFLAG meeting?" It wasn't so much a question as it was a shocking thing for Steph to hear. She did know about the counseling, and she had given her mother the information but she didn't know they had joined the group.

"Yes, dear. He goes twice a week."

"Okay. Well, I will just double check with Julia that she is free on Sunday and if so, we will be there."

"Just let me know, okay Stephy?"

"I will. Talk soon, Mom." Steph hung up the phone and just stood looking at it in the cradle for a few minutes before returning to the living room with Julia.

Steph flopped on the couch, forcing Julia to work to keep from spilling her glass of wine, and pulled a pillow to her chest. She stared at the image on the paused television, but didn't speak.

"Everything okay? I assume that was your mom?" Julia reached out and touched her arm to show her concern.

"So, remember how I asked if you would be okay to meet my parents?"

"Of course I do. It was only last week. Why? Are they actually okay with that?"

"So, how would you feel about meeting my whole family?" Steph shifted to face Julia. "If it's too much, you don't have to. My sisters can be a lot and I'm not sure if it will just be the two of them or if the kids are coming. You can say no," She blurted.

"I would love to meet any and all of your family," Julia chuckled. "So, when is the big event?"

"Sunday?" Steph squeaked.

"Sounds perfect."

***

On Sunday morning Steph arrived at Julia's just after 10. She wanted to make sure they were on time for dinner at 5 sharp, as it always was at her parent's house. It was a couple of hours drive to get there and she didn't want it to seem like they just pulled in when the meal was served.

Julia was wearing pajama shorts and an old t-shirt and still rubbing the sleep out of her eyes when she opened the door and let Steph in. "If you are going to start showing up here at this hour on my day off, I'm going to need to give you something." She smiled and reached into the drawer of the hall table. "I think this will help keep you from waking me at the crack of dawn."

Before Steph looked at what Julia had in her hand she replied, "This is so not the crack of dawn and I just wanted to make sure that we were on time."

"Are you even paying attention to me?" Julia laughed and shook the object in Steph's face. "I had a key cut for you."

"For what?" Steph sounded confused.

"Don't play dumb, for my apartment." Julia shook her head.

"I mean, why did you get me a key?"

"Well, I don't want to rush this, but I did want to show you that not only am I 'meet the parents' serious about you, I'm 'I want to show how much you can trust me by letting you have a key to my place' serious." Julia stood watching Steph be unsure how to react.

"I love you. I'm in love with you. Have I said that? Of course I haven't, but I wanted to. For a long time I wanted to tell you that but it seemed like it was too much, or not enough, or that the words come off as meaningless." Steph rambled as she shuffled through the pockets on the front of her book bag. "I do, though. I love you. More than I think I have ever loved another person. I have never felt this way with anyone else. I mean, I still want to kill you sometimes when you do things to annoy me on purpose, but it never makes me want to be around you or with you any less." Steph continued to fumble through the items in the bag.

"Aha!" She exclaimed as she pulled something out and opened her hand to Julia. "I did the same thing for you. A couple of weeks ago. I was going to give it to you on the day that I moved back into the house, but the timing seemed wrong."

Julia laughed softly and rubbed her eyes again. "Thanks babe. This means a lot. Oh, and I love you too." She leaned in a kissed Steph on the cheek that was still warm from the flush of the panic she had been feeling. "Now, can you please tell me why you are here so freaking early for a 5 o'clock dinner?"

Steph shrugged, "I didn't want to be late."

"Nervous. Got it. Just give me 20 minutes. I'm going to jump in the shower." Julia stretched and headed down the hall to the bathroom.

***

After close to an hour and a half, Julia was finally ready to go. They drove in silence for most of the two hour ride to Steph's parents, but Steph could tell that she wasn't the only one in the car that was nervous about what the evening would bring.

"Is there anything I should tell you before we get there?" Steph had never brought anyone home to meet her family and she wasn't sure what the protocol was.

"What do you mean?"

"I mean, like, there will be a prayer before we eat and there is a lot of religious stuff on the walls when you go in."

"I figured as much. Listen," Julia took Steph's hand. "It's going to be okay. I know we are both a little anxious about this, but no matter what happens, I love you and we are going to be okay."

They pulled into the driveway a couple of minutes later and sat staring at the front of the house. Julia squeezed Steph's hand, undid her seatbelt and opened the passenger door. Steph finally pulled herself back to reality and did the same. She had always stopped at this point of her arrival to her parents' to remind herself to act a certain way and not to get frustrated when they started asking her about settling down and getting married. Now she reminded herself to be as natural as she could be. She needed Julia to see that she wasn't going to change around them. She needed to let them see the real her, no matter what.

Julia stood beside her and intertwined their fingers, watching Steph prepare. "You know, it's getting a little chilly out here."

Steph closed her eyes and gritted her teeth before smiling down at the brunette beside her, "shall we?" She gestured to the front door. "Mom, we're here!" Steph shouted as she opened the door. She could hear the bustle of activity coming from the kitchen.

"You weren't kidding about the artwork," Julia commented, pointing out the large picture of the Virgin Mary that greeted them. "She's so big I could sit on her lap."

Steph laughed despite herself and called again to let her mother know they had arrived. The laughter from the kitchen ceased and they could hear footsteps making their way toward them. The knot in the pit of Steph's stomach was growing as the noise approached and she suddenly feared she would throw up before she could make this introduction.

Steph's mother and her two sisters stopped in the doorway of the porch, all smiles and waiting for her to speak, but she could only stare. Julia watched her, waiting, but decided to take the initiative.

"Nice to meet you all, I'm Julia. You must be Sherri and Jane?" She extended her hand to shake theirs and they nodded.

"Hey. Great to finally meet the famous Julia who caused all the ruckus around here," Jane said, grasping her hand.

"Yeah, life has gotten a little more interesting since I first heard your name, that's for sure," Sherri added.

"Glad I could bring some excitement to your lives?" Julia replied in a questioning tone.

"It's nice to finally meet you properly." Steph's mother shook her hand.

Steph was still standing silently as her mother took their coats and ushered them into the living room. She sat with Julia on the small love seat across from the couch where Sherri, Jane and her mother were getting comfortable.

"First of all, Julia, I feel like I really need to apologize to you for that morning at the house," Mrs. Underwood started, causing Steph's jaw to drop more noticeably than she realized. "I overreacted and I'm slowly learning to accept you both and I feel we need to get off on the right foot. I shouldn't have treated you the way I did and I would like us to start over."

"Ah, oh. Of course," Julia stammered. "Consider it forgotten."

"I think this calls for a drink," Jane piped up, "Steph, you want to give me a hand, let Mom and Julia get to know each other?"

"Sure thing." It was the first words she had muttered since they made it to the house. "Right behind you." Steph smiled at Julia in reassurance and headed into the kitchen.

As soon as they were alone, Jane grabbed her by the shoulders and looked deep into her eyes. "Damn girl. She is beautiful! Even hotter than the last one by my measure. Maybe even hotter than that Valerie girl that was a flash in the pan for you back in the day."

"Huh? How do you know about any of that?"

"I'm not blind, little sister. I have known you were into girls since we were *young*." She held onto the word longer than necessary.

"How could you have? Sure, you as much as pushed me out of your life when we were just teenagers." Steph brushed Jane's hands from her shoulders, stepped back and crossed her arms.

"I regret that. I really do. But I knew and I was afraid you were actually going to tell me. I didn't want to have to keep your secret. It was hard enough with everything I was going through."

"You're my sister! You were supposed to be there for me. What could have possibly been so big in your life that having to deal with me was such an inconvenience for you?"

"It's not important anymore. It probably wasn't all that important then, but it felt like it was the end of the world and the only way I knew how to deal was to push you away." Jane lowered her eyes.

"Fine. Whatever. It would have been nice to have you in my corner though. Maybe if I knew I had some support I wouldn't have been hiding all these years." Steph scuffed her foot across the tile floor.

"Maybe. I'm glad you are out now though and I want you to know that I am always here for you. If you think you could forgive me, that is." Jane pulled a bottle of wine from the fridge and went about lining up the glasses on the counter.

"Of course I can." Steph released her arms and gave Jane a hug. "Now, let's get out there with these drinks so I can rescue my girlfriend from our mother."

EPILOGUE

Almost a month had passed since the dinner at her parents and Steph had never felt lighter. She found herself reaching for Julia's hand at every turn and even allowing a quick kiss before heading into her office in the mornings when they arrived together for work. She wasn't sure when Julia had slept at home last and she wasn't keen for her to do it anytime soon.

She woke first on their day off and watched Julia sleep for a few minutes before setting up a special date in the backyard. A big car chase had kept them both at work for most of the night, so it was mid-afternoon when she pulled herself from beneath the sheets.

The date was nothing fancy, but she knew that Julia would love it. Steph hung a white sheet from the eve of the house and pinned it to the grass with some large stones to create a viewing screen before setting up the projector at the back of the yard and a blanket in the middle for them to watch a movie when it got dark. Truthfully, she had more planned than a movie, but this was the backup plan.

When she was done, Steph crawled back in bed beside Julia and pulled her into her arms. She loved the feeling of the heat of their bodies pressed together and the way Julia held her tighter when she would sigh, or pull her closer if she moved in her sleep. Steph felt contentment like never before just having her beside her. She started running her fingers over Julia's exposed back absentmindedly.

Julia finally opened her eyes and immediately smiled up at Steph. "That tickles."

"Sorry, I didn't mean to wake you."

"Yes you did." Julia stretched. "I felt you leave. Did you make coffee?"

"No. Just set up a little surprise for you for later."

Julia rolled and looked at the clock. "Wow, it's almost supper time. You should have woken me before now. I'm never going to get to sleep tonight." She pulled herself from Steph's embrace and threw on an old t-shirt from the nightstand.

"You needed to sleep. Besides, I can't surprise you if I don't let you stay in bed." Steph pulled up the covers to make it appear as though the bed was made and followed her down the hall to the kitchen.

It was that time of year when the sun went down by 5 o'clock and Steph was watching it in the sky, waiting for the time to bring Julia to the yard. Julia poured them each a cup of coffee and Steph noticed that she had gone from a light smile to a more serious expression. "Can we talk about something?"

The serenity that Steph had been feeling washed away. "Um...okay? Did I do something wrong?"

"No, nothing like that, I've just been wanting to ask you something but it is weird."

"It can't be that weird. What is it?" Steph took her hands.

"Well, I want to ask you to move in with me. But you see, there is this whole thing where I have this stupid rinky-dink apartment that I know you don't want to live in, and it's weird for me to ask you to move in when I am really asking to move in with you." Julia waited but Steph just stared. "I was hoping you would ask me, but it doesn't seem like it is going to happen, so there it is."

Steph started to laugh. She laughed so hard and so long that Julia's confused look became one of concern. When she finally caught her breath, she looked at Julia and smiled. "The big surprise? I was going to ask you to live here. Well, there was more than that, but that was the plan."

Julia pulled her into a hug. "That's amazing. I'm so glad we are in the same place. I love you so much."

"I love you too."

***

Over the next couple of weeks Steph and Julia spent most of their free time either moving Julia's stuff into the house or with Kerri and Summer, helping to put the finishing touches on their wedding plans. They had become a tightknit group of friends and Steph felt like she had found her place.

On the day of the wedding, they took their reserved seats near the front in the back room of Willie's bar and waited for the music to change. Steph could tell that Kerri was nervous, standing at the top of the aisle with her brother Jack at her side. She glanced over her shoulder, out the window to see the door of a car opening and a flash of a white dress as Summer arrived for the service.

Steph looked at Julia who seemed to already be crying and pulled a tissue from her jacket pocket. "Here, you are going to need this."

"Thanks, Grandma. Got some certs in there for me too, or maybe a Werther's to keep me quiet for the ceremony?"

"Ha, ha. Just be grateful that I know you well enough to have brought these along," Steph replied.

As the wedding march began flowing from the keyboard in the corner, they stood to watch Summer make her way toward Kerri. She took Ava by the hand and adjusted her train before making the first step into the rest of her life.

By the time they made it through the vows, the entire congregation was in tears, including the brides. Even the normally stoic Steph could feel a few tears falling down her cheeks. "It's just so beautiful, the way they love each other that much. I hope you know how much I love you."

Julia blushed and gripped Steph's hand. "Of course I do. You show me every day and in every little way possible."

Steph stared at Julia with an adoring smile and whispered, "I think one day that will be us."

Julia squeezed her hand even harder. "I know it will."

FROM THE AUTHOR

This book, even more than the first, was a labour of love. I suffered with imposter syndrome throughout the process, all the while dealing with anxiety and depression that were only exacerbated by the pandemic that threw the world into chaos over the last year. Everything felt impossible, but I persevered with the help of an amazing support system. I learned a lot through all of this, but most importantly, I have learned to love those close to you as hard as you can and cherish every minute you can spend with them, even if it is through a screen.

There are so many people that deserve credit for not only this book, but *Summer* as well. I promise to be brief and only name a few.

I believe it is said that no good book would be worth reading if not for a great editor. (I can't find it said anywhere, so maybe I said it, I'm unsure.) But it is certainly true in this case. AJ Ryan. You are a superb editor, a fantastic sounding board and an even better person. I certainly hope you are the one who is criticizing my work well into the future.

Amanda Labonté. If not for you, these books wouldn't exist. Your willingness to "take a look" at book one started a journey for me that I didn't know I wanted to be on. I also had no idea the kind of twists and turns it would take me through. I blame you for them, but I am grateful for each one.

Matthew LeDrew. There are no words. You are by far one of my oldest and best friends. Thank you for looking past that and listening to Amanda when she said my work might be alright after all. I remember the days when Engen Books was not even in its infancy, just a glimmer in your eye. I admire your work ethic, drive and determination that have turned it into what it is today. Keep getting the voices of talented authors (and me) out there. It is truly your calling.

To my wife, Erica. Thank you for your love, first and foremost as it inspires the love that my characters share. Thank you for your support in every way possible that allows me to live my dream every day. Mostly, thank you for believing in me and what you think I can accomplish. You make me believe in myself and as far as I am concerned, that is OUR greatest accomplishment.

I need also to thank my family. Mom, Dad, Chris, Nan, Auntie and "Uncle" Stan. Although my writing is not necessarily your standard reading not only did you all buy a copy of book one, you all read it. I can't explain here in such a limited space what that support meant to me. I love you all.

Finally, a big thank you for Sarah White and Lenny Benoit who took the time to beta read my first book, the company that laid me off from my job to allow me the time to work on it and all my friends, acquaintances, and those that I have never met who took the time to read my words. I hope you all enjoyed the love.

ON SALE NOW FROM ENGEN BOOKS

ABOUT THE AUTHOR

Sarah Thompson is a former radio broadcaster and journalist from Grand Falls-Windsor, Newfoundland & Labrador.

She was first published in the Engen Books compilation *light | dark* in 2010 with the science fiction story 'Remers.'

In 2020 Engen Books released her debut novel, *The Love of Summer*, to wide success.

Sarah currently owns and operates her own dinner theatre business for which she writes the shows, including *Leroy's Diner, Going to the Chapel*, and, *I'll Be Home For Christmas*.

She is a big fan of the community theatre scene and can often be found performing or directing with the Off Broadway Players. Sarah lives with her wife and dog, Roger, in Corner Brook, Newfoundland.

The Love of Julia is her second novel.